M-81

Emerging Doctors

Willoughby S. Hundley III, MD

iUniverse, Inc.
Bloomington

M-81
Emerging Doctors

iUniverse books may be ordered through booksellers or by contacting:

iUniverse
1663 Liberty Drive
Bloomington, IN 47403
www.iuniverse.com
1-800-Authors (1-800-288-4677)

ISBN: 978-1-4620-0466-9 (sc)
ISBN: 978-1-4620-0467-6 (ebook)
ISBN: 978-1-4620-0468-3 (dj)

Printed in the United States of America

iUniverse rev. date: 3/23/2011

Thanks to Jennifer

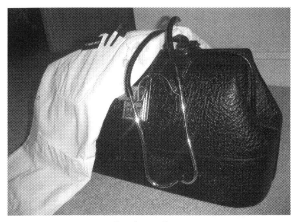

Student Gear

Chapter 1
Ward 63–BS

At six forty-five a.m., the air was already warming. Virginia's summers are usually uncomfortably hot, sticky, and humid, especially in the city. This July Monday in Richmond was no exception. Obie Hardy crossed the intersection as the light turned green and turned into the McGuire Veterans Hospital entrance. He drove slower than the other vehicles entering the hospital complex because he was searching for the parking area designated for medical students. The frequent speed bumps were welcomed, helping conceal his unfamiliarity by forcing him to slow down. After three-quarters of a lap around the complex, he found what he believed to be the appropriate lot and parked his gray-blue Chevette. He gathered his equipment that he had assembled, trying to anticipate any possible need that could arise, since this was to be his first experience at taking care of patients. He donned his white jacket—essentially a short-sleeved, snap-up, smock-like garment he felt was more fitting for a dentist than a physician. Most medical students wore this type of jacket, probably because they were the cheapest and lightweight, and all their pocket references and medical instruments could be carried easily. Obie liked these jackets because they were cool cotton and unpretentious, not wishing to create an image he could not live up to. Outfitted in his jacket, pockets full of paraphernalia, and black bag in hand, he walked up the sidewalk to the Veterans Hospital, Ward 63, Psychiatry.

The McGuire Veterans Administration Hospital, VAH, was typical of the 1940's style government buildings. It could easily have been a post office or high school by appearance; only its overall size implied a greater function. The complex was largely one-story passages connecting two story wards, sometimes fifty yards apart. The buildings spanned lengths of up to half a mile. The ward entrances had cement steps and stoops with waist-high brick walls. The brick exterior had symmetrically positioned, multi-paned windows, wood-framed, with no screens. The institution spread out over about a hundred and fifty acres, including grounds and parking lots.

Obie turned right upon entering and saw John Morgan, a classmate, standing down the hall—a familiar face that might sedate the butterflies in his stomach. John was short, about five feet, seven inches, with short brown hair and a thick mustache. His white jacket was standard medical student uniform. He stood in an almost bowlegged stance, shifting weight from one foot to the other repeatedly.

"Hardy!" he chirped out. "This is the place!" Obie smiled and walked toward him. The floor was white tile with a waxy shine, the walls pale yellow. "Are you on this rotation or here as a patient?"

"I'm not sure," answered Obie. "This is quite a maze of buildings!"

"Yeah. They spread it out like this so that one bomb couldn't take out the entire hospital," John explained. His Blue Ridge Mountain accent gave his explanation a common sense, simple, earthy flavor. He was anxious to get to know Obie. They had been in the same classrooms for two years with 166 other medical students. Since John sat up front and Obie in the back, they hadn't become much more than acquaintances. Different study groups and social patterns had kept them distant. "Put your stuff in the lecture room here," he offered.

The third student, Cheryl Wright, was waiting in the lecture room already. There were a dozen metal, table-like desks with Formica tops in the room, each with a matching chair. A slate blackboard and bulletin board completed the classroom image. Classrooms were familiar to medical students after four years of college and two years of medical science lectures. But now, this was merely a briefing room for them; the real learning was to take place on the wards with real patients. Live human beings would replace the textbook concepts, lecture descriptions, color-slide pathophysiologic images, and therapeutics that comprised their medical education so far.

The attending ward psychiatrist arrived shortly to orient and brief the students. She was a middle-aged woman with graying, dirty blonde hair and a pleasant face, calm and unwrinkled. A motherly radiance emanated from Dr. Andrea Blanton. She outlined the schedule for the six-week rotation, including the drug detoxification unit, outpatient clinic, emergency night call, and the inpatient ward. "Feel free to come by my office and talk any time, especially if you have *any* problems during this rotation. Now I'd like to introduce Dr. Carl Anderson, our second year resident. He'll work closely with you on Ward 63." She beamed at Dr. Anderson and the students, and then faded out of the room, rarely to be seen again during the rotation.

Dr. Anderson was a tall, average-built young man in his late twenties. He had straight, sandy hair and somewhat retracted lower teeth, so that it seemed saliva would drool from the corners of his mouth if he wasn't careful when speaking. With himself, he was fairly secure, but in charge of instructing medical students in psychiatry, he was somewhat unsettled. Each student would take turns doing admission histories and physicals, dictations, and writing orders on the veterans admitted to Ward 63. He would supervise the process and be in charge of morning rounds each day. Since it was Monday (they soon discovered psychiatrists don't work weekends), there were already admissions waiting. He wrote three names and bed numbers on the blackboard and scampered off.

So that's it? thought Obie. *No swimming lessons, life jackets, or kickboards? Jump in and sink or swim!* He tried to picture Dr. Anderson seated on a lifeguard stand with sunglasses, a whistle, and zinc oxide on his nose. No way. He picked up his black bag, wrote down "Leroy King - 20B" on his clipboard, and walked out to the nurses' station to review his patient's chart. The admission sheet supplied the demographics: age, fifty-seven years; race, black; address, Greenville, SC; diagnosis-_____. "What? No diagnosis?" He quickly flipped through the pages of the rest of the chart, all blank.

He walked down the hallway to the ward area, a large open room like a warehouse. There was a wide passage down the center with a four foot-high partitioning walls running left and right to meet the exterior walls, dividing the ward into four sections on each side, each with six beds. The second section to the right, second bed, was 20B. Mr. King's bed was empty, but Mr. King had spotted Obie from the lounge area at the end of the ward and came walking up behind him.

"Mr. King?" Obie inquired.

"Why sure, doctor. Why sure," he answered. He was a short, black man with droopy eyelids and a large grin.

"I'm the medical student who will be working with you. My name is Hardy."

"Why sure. I'm Leroy King."

"I need to talk with you and do a complete physical exam. Can you tell me why you're here?"

"Why sure. I'm depressed." He smiled cooperatively. "It happens to me a lot, 'specially after I been drinking."

"How does it bother you?"

"Voices. I hear voices. They says I'm no good … oughta be dead."

The questioning continued for thirty minutes with little further information exchanged. Mr. King didn't know if his family had any health problems. Possibly he had a reactive skin test for tuberculosis, TB, some years back and he had a morning cough that he attributed to smoking two packs of Marlboros a day.

Each medical specialty has its own specific patient examination routine. Medical students learning to perform physical exams are taught the entire cardiac exam, urogenital exam, connective tissue exam, orthopedic exam, and so forth. Unsurprisingly, students often spend one and a half hours completing a routine physical examination, not knowing which short cuts to take, fearful of missing a diagnostic clue. Obie did a thorough exam and tried to justify in his mind skipping the undesirable rectal exam—without success. It is part of the gastrointestinal exam. He had been taught that there are only two instances where a rectal exam may be excluded: 1- when the patient has no asshole; or 2- when the doctor has no fingers. Mr. King was pleasant and quite cooperative; it shouldn't be too difficult. Obie turned his back to Mr. King, reaching into his black bag for a rubber glove and KY lubricant.

"Well," he said, "we're almost done. We just need to put a finger up in your rectum, and we'll be done."

"Why sure, doctor. Why sure."

He turned to face Mr. King, and found him fully cooperative, with his own index finger placed in his rectum!

Cheryl Wright was in the briefing room when Obie returned to write up his notes. She was an attractive girl with long, straight light brown hair. She was obviously upset, her face flushed and eyes glaring.

"What happened, Cheryl?" asked Obie.

"Mr. Satterwhite in room six," she fumed forth. "Bipolar affective disorder … First, he called me 'nurse' saying, 'How about a date sometime, nurse?'; and, 'I like white women, nurse.' I discussed the case with Dr. Anderson, and he told me to draw a lithium level on him. So I go to this semi-private room, and this six-foot-tall, 230 pound black man is fondling his genitals through his gown. I tell him that I needed a blood sample. He stands up, pulls up his gown, and says, 'I got a vein you can sample, nurse!'"

Obie laughed, and his feelings of uncertainty about his own patient dissipated some. John came in with a chart under his arm and his black bag in hand. "Hi, guys!" he chirped as he walked over to the shelf-like counter that ran along one wall of the room. "They start us hopping right off, don't they?" They affirmed his remark, and he methodically turned to a specific area in the chart and began writing. "Have you done any of your dictations yet? No? Well, the directions are listed by the phone here. You can stop and hold, reverse, edit, or whatever. It goes kind of slow at first." At this, he lifted the phone receiver, dialed some numbers, and began reciting smoothly and briskly. "This is John Morgan, M-81, dictating for Dr. Carl Anderson. Admission history and physical on patient Steven Gardner, patient number 922-17-6505, admitted 7-16-79, Ward 63. Mr. Gardner is a forty-eight-year-old black male paranoid schizophrenic who was well until three weeks prior to admission when …"

Cheryl and Obie looked at one another and then at John, almost bewildered. Their task of appearing as competent medical students would certainly be more difficult now. The sink-or swim-image returned to Obie, but now he was splashing about in the water as John sped by in a motorboat, the waves of the wake splashing upon Obie's face. Cheryl leaned toward Obie, having regained her composure now, and said, "I'd like to draw a lithium level on *him*!"

"Why sure, nurse. Why sure," answered Obie.

Obie found Dr. Anderson in Dr. Blanton's office (Dr. Blanton was not in) and suggested that Dr. Anderson examine Mr. King. Obie explained, "I've only done four physical exams before today, and I'm not sure about some things. I think Mr. King's liver is enlarged, and I'm not sure about …"

"Just write down what you find. I'll co-sign it. Look through his old chart and restart his regular medications. If you have anymore questions, order a medicine consult. I'll sign your orders." Dr. Anderson smiled at him, patted him on the shoulder, and said, "Thanks, bud!"

Obie wandered back to the nurses' station, trying to organize his thoughts and develop a plan of care for his patient. He was apparently on his own; it was up to him to arrange this patient's hospital care. He asked a nurse for the old chart and sat down to decipher it. Incredible! Why hadn't he looked for the old chart before? Up front was a typed synopsis of Mr. King's last admission, a "discharge summary." A plethora of information was there … medications, diagnoses, blood chemistries, X-rays, and more. He had been on several drugs for TB, recommended for a one-year period. He had used an inhaler for his lungs during episodes of colds and was on an anti-depressant. Now Obie easily formulated an admission note and orders, guided by the patient's past management. He doubted Mr. King completed his twelve-month course of TB drugs, but he was concerned about his possible liver enlargement and chose not to reorder these medicines. He could always start them the next day.

Dictating the admission history and physical exam, or H&P, was awkward and took three takes or editings. Now it was late afternoon and, after clearing it with Dr. Anderson, Obie left for home.

Obie arrived at seven thirty Tuesday morning so he could see his patient before eight o'clock rounds. John was in the students' room already, writing in one of three charts he had on the counter. He grinned at Obie, eyes sparkling too brightly for that morning hour, and lifted a Styrofoam cup of black coffee.

"Good morning," he said, "checking the patients' charts before rounds, too, huh?"

"Yeah," replied Obie as he deposited his black bag and books on a desktop. In the nurses' station, he found Mr. King's chart and noted how it looked like a "real" patient chart. There were vital signs, nurses' notes, physician's orders, and lab reports on the pages. The chemistries were reported as bar graphs—as well as numerically—and the liver enzyme graphs were off the top of the page. Obie was pleased that he had not written for the TB drugs and noted that the medical consultant had ordered some sputum cultures, vitamins, and an arterial blood gas. He spoke briefly with Mr. King, who was preparing to go shower, and reported for rounds.

Morning rounds were made by Dr. Blanton, the attending physician, accompanied by Dr. Anderson, the medical students, the head nurse, and the psychologist … quite a crowd. Dr. Anderson had three-by-five index cards on each of the thirty-two patients, imprinted on one end with their nameplates, which were the blue hospital cards with their names and data in raised letters. His brief notes were written underneath this. The group started in the ward, moved down the hall with the six semi-private rooms and communal bathroom, and circled the ward at the opposite end of the hall, filled mostly by patients on the neurology service. The students gave awkward, fumbling presentations of their admissions. John introduced Oscar Smithfield, admitted for decompensation of his paranoid schizophrenia. Several bedsides later, Obie presented Leroy King's case, since his bed was empty at the time. Again, John reported on George Harville, senile dementia awaiting placement in a long-term care facility, i.e. nursing home. Dr. Anderson summarized all the patients in between. Cheryl explained Marvin Satterwhite's problems, bipolar affective—also known as manic-depressive—disorder whose lithium level had fallen to three, subtherapeutic. His dose had been raised, and he would be observed for resolution of his manic behavior. John's third patient was a bizarre man, Jerome Olsen, who was neurotic. He had obsessive-compulsive behaviors and was recently fired and divorced. He shared a semi-private room with an unfortunate patient, Roger Mills. Mr. Mills was a paranoid schizophrenic who became disturbed by any breaks in the routine. He feared that every change was somehow threatening, especially with his new roommate, Mr. Olsen.

"Please, doctor," pleaded Mr. Mills to Dr. Anderson. "Help me!" He was a thin, small white man, middle-aged and unshaven. His eyes appeared desperate, as did his tone.

"Everything will be fine soon," assured Dr. Anderson.

"But … he says he's going to burn up the room!" Mr. Mills said, pointing to Olsen. Mr. Olsen was a black man in his mid-twenties—cool and unshaken. He grinned and shook his head in apparent pity over Mr. Mills's misconceptions. He placed a cigarette in his mouth and, when lighting his lighter, was interrupted by Dr. Anderson.

"Please, Mr. Olsen, we only allow smoking in the lounge."

"Oh. Okay, no problem," he answered and walked off down the hall.

"We've caught him smoking in the room several times," reported the head nurse to Dr. Anderson.

"Well, let's see if this has helped," answered Anderson. As the team moved out of the room, Obie looked back at the frightened Mr. Mills. He was sitting on his bed, but, underneath the springs, a mass of crumpled newspapers had been shoved.

The Ward 63 team gathered in the briefing room, minus the head nurse, who returned to her work on the ward. Treatment plans and questions about diagnoses were addressed. Dr. Anderson's beeper went off, sending him to the telephone. As he hung up, he announced, "The clinic is sending up a patient for admission. Who wants him?"

Dr. Blanton had vanished already. John looked at the other medical students, grinning, his white teeth shining beneath his brown mustache.

"I'll take him," volunteered Obie quickly, before John could expand his patient load. "What's wrong with him?"

"Overtly psychotic. Probably undifferentiated schizophrenia. I've also got a consult in A&D to see."

"What's 'A&D'?" asked Cheryl.

"Admissions and discharges," explained Carl. "It's really an emergency room, but the VA has its own nomenclature."

"Can I go with you?" queried Cheryl.

"Sure. Let's go."

A&D was a good half-mile journey along the corridors of McGuire Veterans Administration Hospital, also known as the VAH, or simply the V.A. They crossed the end of the arcade, the central hub of the complex. Here was the PX store, cafeteria, vending machines, lounge with pool tables, twenty-four-hour banking machine, and auditorium. The main drag was wide with double yellow lines down the center to keep the traffic flowing in appropriate directions. Vehicular traffic included wheelchairs, motorized stretchers for spinal injury patients, and electrically powered scooters or trains for housekeeping and maintenance. They turned left down the corridor toward A&D.

The A&D department was made up of a long room with a desk-high counter at one end and areas for four or five litter type beds along one wall. It was crowded with four patients, nurses, a unit secretary, and a physician.

"Dr. Anderson! Good!" greeted the A&D doctor. "Yours is the one in the back. Some domestic problem had him distraught. He hasn't slept in weeks, is not eating, boozing it up, and now he's threatening violence. He wants to kill someone. I thought it would be unwise to manage him as an outpatient."

"Sounds like an appropriate admission to me," said Dr. Anderson as he took the chart from the A&D doctor. He turned to Cheryl, "Agitated depression." They approached the patient in the far corner bed. "Mr. … ah … Robertson?" he asked after looking on the clipboard for his name. "I'm Dr. Anderson, and this is a medical student … ah …" turning to read Cheryl's name tag, "Wright. Student Doctor Wright."

"I want that son of a bitch that stole my wife!" boomed Mr. Robertson, a muscular man with a squared jaw and brow. "The stinking pig! He's a policeman, I hear."

The opposite wall was metal to about waist height and then glass, mostly covered by curtains. Between the curtains were gaps where one could glimpse people walking by in the hall. A security officer was strolling by; the blue uniform and badge flashing by the curtain gaps caught Mr. Robertson's eye. "Is that the bastard?" he screamed.

Mr. Robertson sat up off the litter and produced a pistol from under the sheet. A crack like thunder exploded, and a glass panel in the wall shattered and crashed to the floor, leaving the curtains shivering, as with fright. There were several short shrieks, ducking, and stooping down; and then a heavy silence hung in the air for several seconds. The short shell shock ended as people began crawling about the floor, frantically searching for cover. There were sobs and mumblings everywhere as people scuffed about, knocking over wastebaskets, chairs, IV poles, and other obstacles. The security officer peeked around the corner to identify the source of the shot.

"There you are, cop! I'll get you, Goddammit!" *Blam!* Another shot rang out, and heads ducked everywhere. Drawn by the disturbance, another security officer came running up the corridor to offer assistance. *Blam! Blam!* Two quick shots sent him diving to the floor as another window panel sent glass fragments raining down. "Where are you, cop?" raged Mr. Robertson.

"Security! Help us, security!" called a woman's voice from somewhere in the opposite end of A&D, beneath the counter desk. The security officers, armed only with nightsticks, looked at each other, suddenly realizing the "cop" image their uniforms portrayed. They wore sky blue dress shirts with badges and officer-type caps. Each looked down at his own chest, the badge gleaming like a target. "Security! Where are you?" As if on cue, the officers began stripping off their shirts, caps, and neckties, tossing the garments as far down the hall as possible while cowering on the floor.

Voices mumbled and whispered throughout A&D, but the people themselves were frozen with fear. Mr. Robertson cried out again, "Valerie? Where are you, Valerie? Is it true about you … and the cop?" Cheryl's eyes widened. What if he were to mistake her for Valerie? Images of Valeries flashed through her mind as she strained to envision this Valerie: a brunette or a redhead, short or fat, or having absolutely no resemblance to her. She was on the floor behind the bed next to Mr. Robertson. Her heart pounded forcefully, and she could feel pulsatile chops in her respirations.

"Your wife, Valerie Robertson. She's out in the parking lot now!" a voice announced. Cheryl recognized the voice as the same woman who had called for security. "I saw her come in to get a Coke a minute ago. I think she got two Cokes from the machine. Is somebody here with her?"

Mr. Robertson had slid off the side of the stretcher bed and stood beside it now. He was dressed only in a hospital gown. His head was cocked slightly to the side, screening all sensory input to identify and react to any threat. "Somebody with her?" he repeated as it registered into consciousness. His body was tense, the pistol gripped in both hands and his knees slightly bent as a racer awaiting the starting gun. The marine insignia tattoo gleamed boldly on his right arm. He sprung from his position in a sprint through the A&D doorway.

The security officers, now in only white T-shirts from the waist up, were coincidentally and strategically crouched in the hall on either side of the doorway. They dove out into the path of this charging bull and became entangled in his arms and legs. The knot of bodies fell into a pile on the floor as the pistol slid off down the corridor, spinning on its side like a pinwheel. After some grunting and straining, the officers had Mr. Robertson cuffed, and a nurse came up and gave him an injection in his right buttock. Cheryl rose to a standing position, her legs shaky, her gaze fixed on the patient she was supposed to admit.

The nurse was about age forty and had a seasoned look. Her manner was sure as she stood up beside the officers, who were still holding Mr. Robertson face down and cuffed. Cheryl admired her composure and her ability to perform her duties in the heat of battle.

"Thanks, Helen. You really helped control this mess!" said one of the T-shirted men.

"Well," she answered in the voice Cheryl recognized that had triggered the dash, "it's the first time I've helped 'Hanes-clothed' officers!"

"Well," said Dr. Anderson, who had remained beside Cheryl throughout the ordeal, but whose presence had been forgotten. "It looks like he'll go to the city jail now. He's too violent to manage here. The state penitentiary psychiatrist will evaluate him, I guess."

"That's fine with me," replied Cheryl.

Obie had taken Walter Murphy to the students' room, since he had only a ward bed and wouldn't talk with people around him. He was a black man, age twenty-four, with a thin, trimmed beard and mustache. He walked around the room constantly, changing directions every two or three steps, to the sides or backward randomly, like a wind-up toy. Obie noted that he approached and faced him whenever he collected a thought well enough to speak, but turned and walked off as his chain of thought was broken. Mr. Murphy looked at Obie face to face, grinning widely, with eyes twinkling. "We can do it! Help me get this, and we can do it!"

"Do what?" asked Obie.

"Anything! I've got *it* figured out! Everything!" He stepped back, looking up at the ceiling—or rather, through the ceiling. He was seeing some vision still invisible to the average person.

"Everything?"

"Yeah!" He approached Obie again. "I'm this close to it all!" He held his thumb and index finger about an inch apart. "It's … it's like … ah … " walking off again, looking up through another part of the ceiling.

"How long has this been happening?" questioned Obie, hoping to direct the interview along the format of a medical history.

"I don't know. A while."

"Do you hear voices?"

"No, man. Don't you understand? This is *it!* I've almost figured *it* out. I've almost got the answer!"

"Have you been on medications before?"

"Yeah … " His face lost some of its sparkle, appearing rejected. "The medicines keep me from thinking. They dull your mind." Obie remembered the mask like-faces of some of the Ward 63 patients on antipsychotics, formerly called the major tranquilizers. He knew what Mr. Murphy was talking about. "Don't let them start those medicines! They don't want me to *know*. I'm so close … just a few more days!"

"We'll see. Maybe a different medicine to help you think better."

"Please! You and me can do *it*! We'll know *it*!" Obie could see his patient wanted no part of drug therapy and was not willing to try a different drug. He was invigorated, energized, and clairvoyant, on the verge of a breakthrough discovery… the secret of the world, maybe the universe, or life and immortality. What if he really was a prophet, a philosopher, about to give birth to a revolutionary idea that could change mankind? Obie suppressed these thoughts, afraid to mention them to the other students or doctors, or they might find that he too was insane.

Wednesday morning rounds followed the same course through the ward, the semi-private rooms, and the few beds in Neurology. In room three, they found Mr. Miller, but his roommate was gone. John explained, stroking his chin and grinning slyly. "Er … Mr. Olsen, it seems, managed to start a fire in the trash can in the room last night. The nurses found a bunch of newspaper and other flammable substances stuffed under Mr. Miller's bed. Mr. Olsen was moved to solitary for closer observation."

Room five was equipped for "solitary," with a windowed door with an exterior lock. It was beside the nurses' station for close observation. No dangerous objects were in the room. It wasn't quite a padded room, but the next closest thing. Now, Mr. Miller seemed more relaxed and making definite progress now that the threat of incineration was gone.

Cheryl appeared composed, oblivious to the previous day's high-noon gunfight at the A&D corral. She had retold the saga several times already, trying to assimilate the learning portion of the experience into her medical training. Outside the doorway to room 6, she announced, "Mr. Satterwhite is on the appropriate lithium dosage now, we hope. He will have a repeat level done this morning." Dr. Blanton and Dr. Anderson gave approving nods and began to walk onward. Cheryl had given a professional report on the patient that had been accepted without further questions. She felt proud and in control of the patient's care. From behind them down the hall came a sudden *crash* as a breakfast tray was accidentally dropped. Reflexively, Cheryl dropped to a squatting position, her head down. Slowly she raised her eyes upward to meet the eyes of the group, her cheeks blushing.

"Shell shock," explained Dr. Anderson as everyone about her laughed.

On the ward, Obie briefly presented Mr. Murphy and the team members nodded understandingly. As they turned to move on, Mr. Murphy winked at Obie, making pleading gestures. Obie knew he was begging for his "mind," to hold off the medications. The order for an injectable antipsychotic medicine, Prolixin, had already been entered, anticipating problems with Mr. Murphy taking pills. Soon Mr. Murphy's developing link with divine knowledge would be severed, disconnecting his mind from its mystical energy source. He would think the simple thoughts of everyday, ordinary people, maybe even more simple due to the sedative side effects of Prolixin.

The group dispersed as it approached the nurses' station at the end of rounds. There was a lady with a clipboard removing a chart from the circular, rotating chart rack. She was average height in build, appearing about fortyish, with salt-and-pepper hair pulled up on the back of her head. She wore a nice dress with medium heels and wire-rimmed glasses and had a pen planted in her hair over her right ear. The absence of white in her attire suggested her position was non-medical. Obie noticed that she had opened Mr. King's chart and was studying it with a slight smile on her face, comparing her clipboard papers to the chart. He walked toward her and read her nametag: "Social services." He wondered what input she may have concerning Mr. King.

"Are you working with Mr. King?" he asked.

"Yep, sure am," she answered. "Let's see … it's August, so he must have been headed north."

"That's right. He said he was coming in from Atlanta. Does he have family here?"

She laughed. "I don't think he has any family now. You see, he lives on the road. When it's hot, he moves north. Then, when it gets cool, he goes south again. When he runs out of money or wants a rest, he 'checks in' at a veterans' hospital. He gets some decent food, dries out from the booze, gets any necessary medications, and has us get his military pension check forwarded to him. Then he can buy some new clothes at the PX here, and he's ready to move on."

"Yeah, but he's psychotic and has a chronic lung condition. He needed to be admitted."

"But why was he admitted to Ward 63? He said, 'I hear voices telling me to kill myself.' Naturally, any potentially suicidal patient has to be admitted. His medical problems aren't severe enough to be hospitalized for. Some guys just say 'I want to kill myself.' It's their ticket in, their admission ticket. Lots of these vets run the circuit of veterans hospitals along the east coast, but what can you do?"

"That's incredible," remarked Obie, becoming enlightened about human nature and resourcefulness. He also felt a little foolish about being used—not so much that he was used, but that he hadn't realized it.

"Anyway, his check should be here by Tuesday, and I suspect you'll see a dramatic improvement in his 'condition' then."

"Yeah, I guess so." She closed the chart, smiled at Obie, turned, and walked off down the hall. Obie wandered into the lecture room, thinking about his patients. One who probably didn't need treatment at all and another who needed it but preferred to live without the mind-altering drugs, to allow his mind to run free, dreaming grandiose dreams and ideas. Psychiatry was a crazy specialty all right. The lecture series second year had been euphemistically entitled "Behavioral Science," since "Psychiatry" conjured up visions of insane asylums and lunatics. The students had made the name more appropriate, shortening it to its initials, BS, a familiar expression used to describe the subject already. Obie sat down at a desk table and opened his BS syllabus of lecture notes to read about the use of Prolixin, Mr. Murphy's medication. Through the adjourning door, a physician was visible seated at the nurses' station. He was recognizable as a physician because of his white coat. His coat was long-sleeved, heavy cotton, and cut like a blazer with white buttons. This was the standard-issue uniform of the Medical College of Virginia (MCV) to all interns and residents. This distinguished them from the medical students and other health-care students who usually wore the smock-like jackets. He was writing in a chart as John wandered up behind, leaned sideways to peer over his shoulder, and returned to the briefing room, grinning.

"He's the medicine consult." John looked at Obie, "He's writing orders on Mr. King."

The physician walked in shortly after John and addressed the students, "Who's got Mr. King?"

"I do," answered Obie.

"His blood pressure has been borderline elevated, but we don't need to treat it yet. Probably from his alcohol withdrawal. You need to get a blood gas on him, though; we need that to assess his respiratory status."

"A blood gas? The lab does that?"

"No! It's an arterial stick. You do it."

Obie envisioned the aorta, the major artery in the body, curling up from the top of the heart and coursing downward. He could see the powerful pulsations transmitted with each heartbeat, swelling and recoiling, straining to keep the pressurized blood harnessed within its walls. An arterial stick? "Well ... I could try, if I had someone show me ... , I guess." Surely the medicine consultant would demonstrate this procedure for him on Mr. King.

"Sure!" quipped the consultant, reaching out for Obie's hand. He placed Obie's index and middle fingers on his wrist. "Feel the radial pulse?" Obie nodded. "You just feel the pulse and locate the path of the artery between these two fingers. Stick the needle in the course of the artery between your fingers, and the pulsations alone will fill the syringe with blood." It sounded simple. "Now, just a few details. You prep with alcohol swabs, put a rubber cap on the syringe, put it on ice, and take it to the lab within thirty minutes. Also, this is an *arterial* stick, so you must hold firm pressure on the puncture site for ten minutes." Obie stared at the consultant doctor, stared past him, repeating the steps in his mind before acknowledging comprehension. He was on the verge of replying when the doctor added, "Oh ... , very important. The specimen must not clot. The syringe should be heparinized."

Obie reviewed the procedure with the doctor, step by step, gesturing the process with his hands. He hoped the doctor would sense his reluctance to do this test, having never even seen one done. "I don't know," he stalled. "Er ... Where are the syringes?"

"No problem," consoled the doctor, walking to the medicine room in back of the nurses' station. "I'll even heparinize the syringe for you." He located a glass syringe and drew up some clear liquid from an injection-type bottle, and then squirted it into the trashcan. "It only takes a tiny amount, just enough to coat the inside of the needle and syringe." He handed the syringe to Obie, said, "See you later," and walked away.

John was listening intensely, smiling brightly, his eyes twinkling. He was eager to master this new technique. "I'll go with you, Obie," he offered, almost bouncing from side to side on his toes.

"Great," replied Obie. The company would be appreciated,

although he felt his performance would be scrutinized. If he failed, John would surely ask to try and would succeed. Obie would be exposed as the incompetent student that he was. He searched for the appropriate lab slip to fill out.

"I'll get you some ice for the specimen, Obie."

"Thanks."

Everything was gathered at Mr. King's bedside, and Obie explained, "We need to get a sample of your blood to measure your oxygen."

"Why sure."

"This must come from an artery in your wrist, instead of your arm. It hurts a little more." Obie remembered anatomically that the nerves traveled alongside the arteries throughout the body. Also, the muscles in the arterial walls can cause painful spasms when injured. He imagined that the stick would be quite painful, but felt that "hurts a little more" would be less alarming to hear. The student doctor would be anxious enough already without alarming the patient. "It'll be quick, if you brace yourself and hold still, okay?"

"Why sure, doctor," answered Mr. King, extending his wrist. Obie had Mr. King sit in a chair with his right wrist extended off the front of the armrest. He felt the bounding, strong pulse. He cleaned the skin with alcohol swabs, found the pulse again, cleaned his own fingers with alcohol, felt for the pulse again, and cleaned the skin with alcohol again. He picked up the syringe and felt like he was holding a spear, poised to thrust into the invisible target pulsating between his fingertips.

"You'll feel a stick, now. Try not to move!" He jabbed the needle through the skin without even a twitch from Mr. King. He paused to assure the location of the artery and pressed the needle deeper into Mr. King's wrist. A bright red color filled the hub of the needle, and the glass plunger rose upward in pulsating jerks. Obie's fingers froze in their position, afraid of losing his arterial tap, until the syringe filled with the vivid red blood. He pressed the gauze pad over the wound and held it firmly, realizing that he needed another hand to purge and cap the syringe. John jumped in.

"Let me do that for you, Obie." He took the syringe, purged it, capped it, and placed it in the bag of ice. "I'll run this to the lab for you."

"Okay, thanks," answered Obie, although he was reluctant to part with his treasured specimen. His fingers trembled now that the tension eased. He watched the clock for twelve minutes before releasing his grip on Mr. King's wrist and was only comfortable then after heavily taping down the gauze pad. His fingers ached from the long posturing, and he was reminded from below that he had intended to visit the toilet after rounds. Having resisted the urge to move his bowels for two hours, he now felt some discomfort.

Once in the restroom, he removed his jacket, heavy with instruments and notebooks in the pockets. A chance to relax a moment, in private, not having to look like a doctor or an industrious M-81 student for a brief while. Removing the weighted coat lifted the burden of responsibility, an escape from the demands of the ward. He sighed softly as he sat down for full relief, peaceful.

The door burst open. "Obie?" called John's voice. "There you are! The lab called. They couldn't run the blood gas. It was clotted!"

McGuire Veterans Administration Hospital building

Chapter 2
Group Therapy

Dr. Harold Hensley was a tall, slender man with silver, wire-rimmed glasses. He had a shaggy mustache and dirty blond hair that appeared just that: dirty. His loose-fitting clothes exaggerated his slim physique, giving him a rather gangly appearance. Dr. Hensley was a PhD psychologist. He was the unlikely leader of the patients gathered in group-therapy meetings on Tuesdays and Thursdays. Dr. Hensley would often accompany the medical team on rounds, especially on the days of therapy sessions.

This Thursday session was attended by Obie, anxious to observe his patients undergoing psychotherapy. There were eight men present, seated in the table-like desks. Dr. Hensley sat in front, facing the group like a schoolteacher. He looked at the clipboard in his lap intermittently for patients' names and previous notations. The discussion was to be random, exploring individual

21

thoughts and self-awareness. The room was silent, except for Mr. King, who was humming as he paced about the back of the room, reading the notations posted on the wall and bulletin board and the titles of the books lying in the back of the room. He wore a clean, crisp white shirt, obviously a recent commissary purchase. He indeed had progressed since his check arrived that Tuesday.

"Mr. King? Could you sit down, please, and join the group?" asked Dr. Hensley.

"Oh, I'm fine now. Sure. I'm fine. Go ahead with your session." He stopped humming for a while, and there was complete silence. Dr. Hensley cleared his throat, . . . checked his clipboard, … and looked over at Mr. Murphy.

"Mr. Murphy. Can you tell us what you're thinking about now?"

Mr. Murphy had been staring at his desktop, head bowed. He continued his downward gaze, quiet, only blinking occasionally. The lively sparkle now gone from his eyes, he slowly raised his head and looked toward Dr. Hensley. His gaze was distant and vacuous. He stood up, turned and left the room without speaking. As the door clicked softly closed behind him, Mr. King called out, "Amen!"

"Mr. King, it would be most helpful if you would sit down and join us."

"My arthritis is better when I keep moving. I'm here and doing fine. Amen!"

"You shouldn't disrespect the Lord," came an unsolicited, spontaneous comment from another patient. He was an unshaven Caucasian with scraggly brown hair and a serious look in his eyes.

"Why sure. I love the Lord."

"What do you know about the Lord?" the other patient continued.

"Know ye the Lord, He is God: it is He who hath made us and not we ourselves. We are His people and the sheep of His pasture."

"So, you know the one hundredth psalm."

"Why sure. I know the Bible, the word of God!"

"What about Yahweh?" asked the man. Obie recognized the name from his religion class in college. He realized that the man was educated in religion and was confronting Mr. King. People cling tightly to their religious beliefs, especially during periods of stress. The patients in the room were all psychiatrically impaired or emotionally stressed, or both. They were plants that were uprooted, desperate for sustenance and the stability of the earth. This man was shaking free the last particles of soil still clinging to their roots. Mr. King looked back at the man, composing a response.

"Well, … I only believe in the God of the Bible. None of that Buddha or Muslim stuff!"

The man kept a steady, unblinking gaze. "Yahweh is the God of the Old Testament."

Mr. King stared at the man, afraid to answer and possibly show his ignorance on the subject. The man turned away, facing the front of the room, having lost interest in the unstimulating conversation. Mr. King continued to stare vehemently at the back of the man's head. Again, the room was heavily silent.

Dr. Hensley broke the silence, "Mr. King, please take a seat, and let's change the topic."

Mr. King turned his intense gaze to Dr. Hensley and retorted, "I'm fine now. I don't need anymore therapy. Sure." He walked out the door, but his last words could be heard fading off down the hall, "… and though I walk through the valley of the shadow of death, I am not afraid. For Thou art with me …"

Several people shifted positions in their seats, cleared throats, and looked about the room. Dr. Hensley tried to prompt discussions. "Mr. Smithfield, can you tell us about your job? What kind of work do you do?"

"Ah … auto body shop."

"Do you enjoy your work?"

"It's okay."

Silence.

"How about you, Mr. Mills? Where do you live?"

"Colonial Heights."

"Did you grow up there?"

"Yeah."

Silence.

Finally, the group was dismissed. Obie asked Dr. Hensley about his evaluation of the proceedings.

"Communication was just poor today. I can't see much progress in the group in this session, maybe Tuesday." Obie had drawn a similar conclusion, but wanted his preceptor's professional analysis of the session. Obie was relieved that a fight had been avoided.

Friday morning rounds were fairly productive; several patients were being discharged, Mr. King included. Others were to go out on weekend passes. This was less apparent during the student's first week, but almost blatant now. The more patients that were discharged or out on pass, the easier it was for the doctor on weekend call to make rounds. Hence, a mass exodus developed each Friday. Hopefully, no patient was sent out on pass prematurely so that treatment would be jeopardized in any way. The previous week, Mr. Satterwhite had received a one-day pass, and, during morning rounds the next day, the nurse reported that he had been seen in the hospital parking lot enjoying oral sex with an unidentified female. When questioned about this, he had replied, "Well, Dr. Hensley told me to go out and get a 'job.'"

After rounds, Obie went searching for Mr. King to discuss his discharge and follow-up care. He saw a crowd of patients in the lounge at the far end of the ward. As he approached, he discerned some ongoing discussion and paused curiously outside the doorway to listen. The "Yahweh" man was talking. "The Bible is more widely translated and read than any other man written document in the world. It establishes a moral standard that goes beyond political, social, geographical, and racial boundaries. A universal standard."

"Sort of like last night's beauty pageant," responded Mr.

King. "Each country has its own ideas of what's beautiful, but the Miss Universe Pageant sets a standard of beauty that we alls recognize."

"Yeah, I reckon so," answered Yahweh man.

"They kept saying that Donny Osborn was a real boy-next-door type. The perfect host for the pageant," said Mr. Smithfield.

"He reminds me of a guy that lived down the street from me in Colonial Heights," added Mr. Mills. "We weren't in the same groups of friends, but he was all right."

Mr. Smithfield nodded. "I know what you mean."

"My mother was a churchgoing woman," began Mr. King. "She raised me by the Bible. I don't guess I ever lived up to her Christian standards."

Obie smiled silently. The picture of a group therapy session that he had envisioned was unfolding spontaneously in the TV lounge—unstructured, undirected, and unobserved by therapists. The soul-sharing and mind-searching were progressing naturally. Obie turned and walked away. He could talk with Mr. King later, … after his group therapy.

The second two-week period of the rotation through Psychiatry had Obie scheduled for outpatient clinics in the afternoons. The clinic was where Ward 63 patients returned for follow-up care, along with other patients not requiring hospitalization. Dr. Ischman was the attending physician for the clinic. He was an olive-skinned Indian with short, black hair and a mustache. His age was about forty. He had an average build, and was neatly dressed in a dark necktie and crisp, white jacket. He was quite articulate, with an accent flavoring his speech.

"Now you have an opportunity to see how these patients function in society," Dr. Ischman began, his eyes appearing as black marbles, deep and rich. His movements were smooth and confident, appearing as if preprogrammed, like the computerized animation figures at Walt Disney World. His attire was unflawed, without wrinkles, stains, or any sign of wear. Obie imagined he had no bodily defects, no hidden warts, scars, or even a mole. "It is incredible how many common, unskilled laborers can maintain a functional existence with IQs below 80. They can be productive in structured settings where the work is repetitive or someone tells them what to do. The military is ideal for these people; an officer gives them orders to execute, no problems. When their abilities to think are stressed, overloaded, they can decompensate." Obie could picture a janitor, repetitively sweeping the floor and following a pattern, cleaning the ashtrays and bagging the wastebaskets. How many of such people had low IQ levels? How many everyday people were borderline retarded? He began wondering what Dr. Ischman's IQ level was.

IQ, the abbreviation for "intelligence quotient," is the mental age divided by the chronological age. Someone whose mental and physical age correlate exactly would have a ratio, or IQ, of 1.00, reported as "100", the average or normal IQ. Was Dr. Ischman's IQ 110, or 115, or even 130? What, indeed, was Obie's own IQ? 105, or 120?

The first patient was a woman, unusual for the Veterans Administration system, but not unusual for psychiatry, Behavioral Science. Obie's BS patient experience to date had been all-male, a skewed view of a specialty where two thirds of the patient population is female. They entered the exam room where Mrs. Kelly awaited, a neat but plainly dressed, middle aged woman. In contrast to Dr. Ischman's manner, her movements were jerky and fumbling. Obie guessed her IQ to be in the 86 to 92 range. She was still having difficulty sleeping but reported having less crying spells and nervousness. Dr. Ischman increased her medication slightly and asked her to return in three weeks. As she exited down the hall, he explained to Obie, "Depression is the most common problem we see here. More women present for treatment as it interferes greatly with their day to day life functions. There are probably an equal number of men with depression but they tend to keep their feelings and symptoms bottled up. They often don't seek medical attention until something forces them to. They get fired, their wife leaves them, they punch their boss … those kinds of things. Our society accepts that as being more normal, masculine behavior than telling a beer buddy or a doctor that he hasn't been sleeping well and cried during the late show."

They repeatedly walked in and out of the two exam rooms, occasionally entering Ischman's office to look up something, write up a chart, or just sit down for a moment. Between seeing patients, Dr. Ischman continued his treatise on depression. He summarized the known biochemical and hereditary factors leading to depression, the signs and symptoms, diagnostic tests, long-term prognosis, and medical therapies. He even traced the evolution of drug therapy, revealing how the antidepressants were originally developed as antihistamine medicines for allergies and colds. Their antidepressant activity was coincidentally discovered, and patients taking these medicines for depression are now plagued with the side effects of antihistamines, such as dry mouth, blurred vision, and sedation. Obie found this story particularly helpful in remembering the side effects of these drugs.

Dr. Ischman narrated to Obie during patient breaks throughout his rotation in the clinic. He told how early psychiatry was awkward and imprecise, flavored by the mystic. There were no effective treatments, so patients afflicted with disorders of the mind were separated from society and put away in asylums. Behaviors were controlled physically with restraints, straightjackets, rubber rooms, and barred windows; chemically with sedatives; and surgically with lobotomies and electric shock treatments. Medical research in the area of the brain and behavior lagged immensely behind all other areas. The brain is such a complex organ, and nerve cells, among the few types of tissue cells unable to multiply, are capable of only minimal regeneration. Also, studies conducted on animals, due to their lower levels of brain development, are difficult to apply to humans.

A psychiatric evaluation centers on the mental-status exam, the specialty exam of psychiatry. Learning to perform the mental status exam is a difficult task for a student. Making sense out of the results is overwhelming. How does one make use of answers to questions like, "What does 'A stitch in time saves nine' mean?", or "Subtract seven from one hundred, and then subtract seven from that"? There are no yes/no or true/false answers where a negative response to a particular question diagnoses schizophrenia. It's not that simple.

Dr. Ischman sat in his desk chair, holding a clipboard in his lap. "There are seven parts to the mental status exam, right?"

Obie agreed and began naming them, "Intellect, memory, judgment, mood … thought … and …"

"Orientation and affect," completed Ischman. "All psychiatric illnesses match specific parts of the mental-status exam." He labeled the components of the mental-status exam in a vertical column on the clipboard paper. "First," he continued, "'orientation.' What impairs orientation? Orientation is one of the last things affected by dementia—except for, say, concussions. If it is impaired in a young person, it is almost always drug-induced, toxic. In an elderly patient, either *severe* dementia, drug-induced, or toxic-metabolic, such as diabetic complications. It's easy to check for diabetes and do a drug screen. If negative, it's severe senile dementia or Alzheimer's dementia."

He continued, matching the vertical column of mental status elements with the expanding horizontal row of diseases. Disorders of intellect, mental retardation … disorders of memory, dementia … disorders of thought, schizophrenia … and so forth. Several disorders overlapped more than one area of the mental status exam but, still, the chart displayed a simple, systematic approach to psychiatric diagnoses. Obie had listened to hours of lectures in dark classrooms by "teachers" of BS. Dr. Ischman had simplified that mass of BS in a twenty-minute chat, producing a simple chart that could easily be memorized or carried and applied with minimal effort.

The antipsychotics used for schizophrenia have certain side effects. Usage over long periods of time leads to trembling of the hands, similar to Parkinson's, and uncontrolled movements of the tongue and mouth. Short-term use can cause muscle stiffness, where joint movements feel jerky like a ratchet wrench. Mr. McNeil demonstrated this stiffness reaction. Obie was familiar with Mr. McNeil from Ward 63. He was a paranoid-schizophrenic patient, frequently tormented by voices calling to him. He had gone home on pass the previous weekend, somewhat prematurely, but hastened by his brother's recent death more so than the approaching weekend "discharge-and-home-pass" rush. The funeral was on that Saturday.

John Morgan reported on Mr. McNeil on Monday morning rounds, having had emergency call that weekend. "He did well for the funeral but panicked afterwards. He was afraid he would start hearing the voices again and took two extra pills. He got a little stiff, tense feeling which frightened him even more, so he took a couple of more pills. Anyway, he showed up in A&D Saturday night as stiff as a board. He could hardly bend at the waist or turn his head to the side." John animated his presentation, holding his arms outstretched by his sides, with his neck and trunk stiffened like Frankenstein. Obie pitied Mr. McNeil, institutionalized again, having failed his brief trial in the real world. This was not as much due to his schizophrenia but a medication reaction, a reaction resulting from his fear of what might happen. Existence in unsheltered society was so frightening that people with poor coping mechanisms often end up returning to the structured environment of an institution.

Night call was a requirement for students. John had taken his emergency psychiatric call at the VA, but most students accompanied the psychiatric resident on call downtown at MCV. Obie reported to the resident on call Friday afternoon, meeting him in the psychiatric library on the seventh floor. Dr. Joe Kim was a second-year resident, fresh out of internship. He was somewhat short and Polynesian, possibly Filipino. He was also quiet and withdrawn, although this failed to mask his insecurity with his role as the psychiatrist on call. Obie sensed that if there were not much action, Dr. Kim would not bestow upon him a plethora of psychiatric insights during their conversations. Still, he was fulfilling his assignment, following Dr. Kim as he okayed sleeping pill and anxiolytic orders for inpatients that the nurses paged him about.

Finally, about midnight, Dr. Kim was paged to the Blue ER. MCV had six emergency rooms, the Blue ER being for major medical problems. There was a young man there who was acutely psychotic.

The Blue ER was a brightly lit, open area somewhat like a warehouse. It was square, with stretchers along three sides. At the center was a glass-walled room with countertops holding reference books, medical records folders, chart forms, telephones, and other such objects. It was the central hub where staff could look about and visually monitor the ER patients. On the far side, past the glass room, in a dimly lit area, they found their patient, physically restrained, all four extremities tied down to his stretcher. Obie appreciated the similarity to the rack used in medieval torture and wondered if that was why these cots were called "stretchers." The patient was tense and exploded sporadically with inappropriate outbursts, cursing and threatening onlookers. Dr. Kim and Obie timidly approached as the two security guards in attendance stepped back from the stretcher.

"Sir, I'm Dr. Kim. Can you tell me where we are now?"

He strained, trying to sit up against the resistance of his secured wrists, and looked at Dr. Kim. "We're in the fucking bus station, okay? I gotta get outta here! I need a goddamn ticket!"

"Do you know what day it is?"

"Tuesday. It's Tuesday. All right?"

"All right. Now I'd like you to do some thinking for me now. Can you tell me what one hundred take away seven is?"

"You're gonna get seven years of bad luck if you don't get your ass outta here!"

"I want to help you."

"All the help I need is to get these fucking ropes off my hands!" He clenched his teeth and reared up against the restraints

30

again.

Obie stood behind Dr. Kim and could hear the security guards' quiet conversation. He heard the mention "angel dust" and both nodded knowingly, looking back at the patient. Obie was confused by the unstructured situation, a Polynesian doctor, the brightly lit ER, the combative cursing patient, and the whispering of the security guards. Dr. Kim retreated from the patient, withdrawing to the glass hub area to organize his notes. Obie followed, hoping this purposeful action would create some order to matters. Dr. Kim remained silent, reading his notes and the patient's clipboard. He asked Obie to see if the toxicology report was back yet, and Obie gladly left.

He found the computer printout of the drug screen results. It was positive for nicotine and alcohol, but angel dust, PCP, was not listed. He returned to Dr. Kim and posed a question.

"Would the drug screen show angel dust, PCP?"

Dr. Kim did not look up from his paperwork. "Uh ... PCP? ... I ... er... I don't know." He continued studying the chart as if the question was insignificant.

"How about marijuana?"

"Uh ... I'm not sure."

Obie's input seemed unwelcomed, so he wandered away and phoned the toxicology lab. They answered his questions; they could test for marijuana if a cannabis level was requested, but a rapid assay for phencyclidine, PCP, was not yet available. He glanced over at Dr. Kim as he hung up and saw he was still studying his chart work. He walked over to the reference book area and opened Harrison's *Principles of Internal Medicine* textbook. The symptoms of hallucinogen intoxication matched what he had seen in this patient. The treatment was sedation, using an antipsychotic drug if the patient was psychotic or "out of touch." Something struck a familiar note. Dr. Ischman's psychiatric disease table came back to him! If orientation is "impaired in a young person, it's almost always drug induced, toxic." This patient wasn't just out of touch with reality, or psychotic; he was disoriented! Toxic! The security guards were right, probably PCP.

Obie watched the patient for a while, noting that he would rest quietly for spells, but then look around, confused by his surroundings. Finding himself tied down, he would then struggle vigorously against the restraints, crying out loudly. The security guards had wandered off, probably out of boredom and reassurance that the restraints were secure. Obie approached the patient again, speaking calmly, orienting the patient to his surroundings. The patient writhed about still, but each time, Obie repeatedly told him where he was and what was happening. It grew easier to soothe him after each outburst. His behavior slowly became more rational, and, as it did, he pleaded with Obie to untie him.

"We have to keep you restrained to keep you from hurting yourself or other people," explained Obie. "You've been acting violently, thrashing around."

"I'll act okay if you'll untie my hands. Please? … I'll be fine."

Obie didn't respond; he just stood by the stretcher in silence.

"Pssst … hey buddy!" he whispered at Obie. "Come on. Untie my hands, okay?" He looked so sincere. Obie wanted to help him. He looked about for possible reinforcements or directions. No one was aware of their presence in the ER. Obie wondered what to do. He felt sure that, if the patient went wild again, he would be able to grab and restrain one arm by himself. The terror of the thought of releasing this volatile patient caused Obie to tremble in his arms and legs. He hardly believed he was actually considering this action.

"Yeah, buddy. Untie me," he pleaded. Obie's temples pounded; had he begun to trust this patient? His hands were shaking and weak as he raised them up and reach toward the wrist restraint.

"Hey!" interrupted Dr. Kim. "Don't mess with him! He's being admitted to Medicine. Psych will be consulted. Let's go upstairs." Obie looked up at Dr. Kim and felt a warm wave of relief and embarrassment flow over him as the reality hit him.

This wasn't the classroom anymore.

As confusing as the encounter had been, Dr. Kim's presentation at morning rounds surpassed it. The attending physician drilled him in front of the other residents on the specifics of the mental-status exam. How were his abstract thought and cognitive functions? How was his memory, his mood, and was he hallucinating? The only finding Dr. Kim could report on this wild primate that had his limbs bound was that he was "disoriented" and "uncooperative." Obie judged Dr. Kim's IQ to be 95. He couldn't decide on that of the attending.

Back at McGuire VAH later that day, Obie attended psychiatric "grand rounds," where a learned physician from Texas was the guest speaker. His field of expertise was schizophrenia. After his lecture, John Morgan presented the case of a long-term Ward 63 patient, Mr. Lenon. He was paraplegic, paralyzed in both legs, and sat in a wheelchair. His jaw was squared and firm, not softened by his short, gray-highlighted beard. He was a dark-skinned, muscular black man with eyes like black marbles. During a bout of depression, his frail mother watched helplessly as he leapt from her second-story window in a suicide attempt. The shrubbery broke his fall, so he climbed the stairs and jumped again. This time he succeeded in landing on the front walk and fractured his spine.

Obie had noticed the gentleman's flat affect and apparent grasp of the consequences of his actions … since he had been determined enough to make a second death leap. He also felt sympathy for this man who had been depressed enough to attempt suicide twice while his body was intact. Now he was paraplegic, enough to send anyone into the throws of depression.

After the presentation, the visiting expert on schizophrenia conducted a brief interview of Mr. Lenon.

"Did you hear voices? … Telling you to jump out the window?" he asked.

"I don't know. I guess I did," he answered flatly.

After several further questions, Mr. Lenon was excused while the schizophrenia expert elaborated on this case of "schizophrenia" and how he should improve on antipsychotics instead of antidepressants. John Morgan was not convinced of the expert diagnosis, based on a cursory interview of leading questions.

"Are schizophrenic patients usually violent or suicidal?" he asked.

"Well, no, not usually," countered the expert, returning quickly to his elaboration on therapeutics.

"Hasn't electroconvulsive shock therapy been successful in resistant depression?" John continued.

"Sure … but that's not my area of expertise. Now, I would select an antipsychotic with the least long-term tardive dyskinesia effects."

John exchanged glances with Obie and Cheryl, who, having listened to professors lecturing for six years since high school, realized the narrow-mindedness of this expert and were glad he was not their psychiatric attending on Ward 63. Even clinical neophytes were aware that psychiatry was advancing beyond Mellaril and Haldol, major tranquilizers now called antipsychotics. John spoke to the M-81 studs after the "teaching" rounds.

"You know, Mark Twain once said 'Some people are educated beyond their intelligence.'"

"There's a thin line between schizophrenics and those who specialize in treating schizophrenics," added Cheryl.

"We have IQ tests for intellect. Too bad we haven't developed one for common sense," noted John.

"A CQ," said Obie. "Maybe we should start one."

"That's probably why some mediocre med students from the first two years of classrooms excel in clinical rotations; applying knowledge," said John. Obie hoped this was his case, since he was a mediocre med student so far.

He remembered his childhood friend, Charles, who had showed him exceptional common sense. He had taught him, not to go squirrel hunting until all the leaves had fallen; it's easier to track rabbits right after it stops snowing. Charles probably had a CQ of 140. He recalled one evening when they were fourteen. Charles had recruited Obie to investigate a little-used warehouse where used lawnmower parts were junked or stored. He was looking for a Briggs & Stratton carburetor for a three horsepower engine. The dim dusk light concealed their entrance through an empty window frame. When a county sheriff's car passed and slowed down, Charles led the exit and said, "Don't run! He'll think we did something wrong."

They slipped out the window frame and pretended to be looking in from the outside when the deputy walked up. The deputy looked over the unsecured, motor junk pile and assessed that no harm was done. They received only a suggestion not to do that again without the owner's permission.

Friday night, while sipping a glass of wine, Priscilla asked, "What're you thinking about?" Obie, across the table from her, had asked her out to the Garden of Joy restaurant on Belt Road to celebrate the end of the BS rotation. They had ordered a bottle of Piersporter wine, and he was a glass ahead of her. She was a bright girl Obie had met just before college graduation. Her IQ probably 110 to 115, he imagined—CQ an even 100.

"Just thinking about some things I did with Charles growing up," he smiled.

"So, you start OB Monday. What will your night-call schedule be like?"

"I haven't a clue," Obie stated, taking a spoonful of wonton soup. For six weeks at the VA hospital, he had been isolated from other classmates and had no hint of what was next. As he sipped the wine, he felt his IQ slipping 10 to 15 points, becoming relaxed. Alcohol likely suppressed CQ as much as, or more than, IQ level.

Thinking that he might get lucky later, Obie returned to the restroom, remembering the condom machine he had seen there. He put two quarters in the glow-in-the-dark dispenser and turned the knob clockwise. He heard the coins drop inside, but no product was dispensed. He hit the side of the machine with no additional results. Finding another two coins in his pocket, he tried the French-tickler machine—another dud. Wondering whether to go ask for change and try the last machine, he recalled the definition of insanity: repeating the same activity and expecting a different outcome. He returned to Priscilla, knowing he had no preparation for sexual activity.

"You're staying with me tonight, right?" she offered as he drove toward her apartment on Dunston Avenue.

"Sure! You think I'm crazy or something?"

"Well, sometimes I wonder about your IQ."

"Well, after the wine and all, I think it's 69 tonight."

MCV East Hospital Obsetics ER, "The Pit"

Chapter 3
The Pit

Obstetrics and Gynecology, OB-GYN, was the second clinical rotation for the students who began M-3 year in BS. Eighteen students were gathered for the orientation lecture. Obie was quite familiar with the faces of his classmates here, since it was the same group he had sat with during BS orientation, lectures, and exam. He wondered briefly how this set of students had been selected from the class. The names were not alphabetically related, as his cadaver and anatomy partners had been. Also, the academic standings were varied, with a mix of students from upper- and lower-class rankings. He had always felt, and hoped, that he was about in the middle third, an average student. Receiving grades under the pass/fail system made it difficult to figure one's academic rank. This was designed to defuse the intense competitiveness fostered in undergraduate schools, the desperation to achieve a 3.5 or a 3.8 average. In reality, there was little difference, since the "Pass/Fail" grading system had subcategories corresponding to the "alphabetic" system: Pass- Honors equals A; High Pass equals B; Pass equals C; Marginal equals D; Fail equals F. Obie's classroom work had produced straight Ps, so he figured he was a C student. This was humbling for a student who was in the top ten percent of his graduating classes in both high school and college. Obie had always felt he was one of the best students, but now, in med school, he was "average". Rationalizing this by believing he was average among the best college graduates in the state—and beyond—had nudged his ego a bit. John Morgan had helped brighten his image of mediocrity by cheerfully reminding him to think of the formula "P = MD". He had also asked Obie, "What do they call the person who graduates last in the med school class?"

"I don't know. What?" Obie responded.

"Doctor."

It was true. Patients would never know what class rank a physician had, only that he or she was their "doctor."

Dr. Gerald Phanton, head of OB-GYN at MCV, addressed the group. He was a man of modest stature, dark complexioned with flowing black hair. His voice was soft and soothing, yet a depth and seriousness was conveyed as he spoke.

"The patient's modesty and self-respect *must* be preserved at all times. Even the most minor ailment in the reproductive system can be quite frightening to a woman. Always have another female present whenever you examine a woman, for your own legal protection, and always ask permission to perform an exam. Most patients will appreciate your interest in their problem and readily consent to your exam.

"Again, keep a sheet over the patient whenever possible, make sure the door is closed during physical exams, and minimize the number of people present during the exam. Respect and maintain modesty.

"You are in a privileged position with these patients. They will be exposing a portion of themselves that they shield from even close relatives. They feel an enormous vulnerability at this time, understandable when you consider the genitals have some of the densest concentrations of sensory nerve endings in the body. Keep this in mind."

Obie held females in the highest esteem already. Throughout his south-side Virginia childhood, he was surrounded by gentlemen opening doors for ladies, removing their hats when in female company, standing when a lady entered the room, and always addressing them with "Ma'am." Four years in an all-male college engendered a sincere appreciation of female companionship as well.

"Also, physicians must be nonjudgmental. Patients come here for health care, not moral judgments. You must put aside personal prejudices against multiple sexual partners, homosexuality, interracial relationships, and unusual sexual practices.

"There is also a mass of ignorance about the female reproductive anatomy among the general public. This may border on the ridiculous at times, but remember the place of the medical profession; health education and preventive health maintenance. The misconceptions, beliefs, and myths about the sexual organs are endless."

Obie remembered his high school classmates discussing females, stories of sex during wartime where VD was rampant. It was rumored that sergeants told their corpsmen before leave times to field-check a woman by getting some earwax on his finger and inserting it in the vagina during foreplay. Supposedly, if she were infected with clap or syphilis, this would irritate the mucous membranes, causing a burning sensation. If intercourse was inevitable, at least the proper precautions, i.e. rubbers, could be exercised. Obie wondered if such advice was ever "government-issued" but felt it would have been beneficial regardless of its validity, since a man fully aroused is more likely to stick his penis places he would never stick his finger. Hence, if it's too nasty to touch, it's too nasty to screw. High school adolescent "men", unacknowledged virgins, were locker-room and toilet experts on sex. One expert could tell which girls were on the rag; another explained how he could make a girl come using only three inches of his organ, and a black philanderer claimed white girls were a problem for him because they always urinated at orgasm.

Now, after six years of training in science and biology, Obie was certain these stories were untrue … or at least probably not true. He remembered reading in *The Making of a Surgeon* (by William Nolan), where a display board was mounted in a back room off of the ER. It held an array of objects and utensils that had been removed from the rectum, vagina, or penis of patients. It boggled the imagination—Coke bottles, swizzle sticks, pencils, carpentry tools, and some fruits and vegetables.

Rotation schedules were passed out, and the students studied them intensely to find out which nights they were on call. It was inconvenient to come to school the first day of a new rotation, not knowing whether you would be going home that evening or the following afternoon, since the call schedules were not distributed beforehand. Obie was to begin in the clinics and wasn't on call until the third night. Four students each night were on call to follow obstetrical patients through labor and delivery. Obie noted that his call group included John Morgan, Walter Ferguson, and Jim Beam. His first clinic, however, was that afternoon at a city health department clinic.

Obie set out for the clinic on his bicycle, a blue twenty-inch, girls' three-speed with the seat and handlebars raised to the max. It was a scratch-and-dent floor model he had found for under sixty dollars. His budget could have been stretched to acquire a nicer model, but the prior loss of one bike to the inner-city crime force tempered any desire for extravagance. Obie didn't mind the awkward appearance of riding such a bike if it might discourage potential thieves. He was glad that the clinic was within biking distance from MCV, on North Twenty-fifth Street. It was also along his route home. He pedaled down O Street until reaching North Twenty-fifth Street and found the Richmond City clinic.

This was a family-planning clinic staffed by two OB-GYN residents, one male and one female. They seemed surprised to see a med student there. The male resident said, "I'm amazed that they keep this as part of the students' rotations." His complexion was dark, and he had wiry, short, black hair and a neatly trimmed beard. Turning his gaze to the female resident, he peered over the top of his wire-rimmed glasses that sat low on his Roman nose and addressed her, intentionally loud enough for Obie to hear the conversation. "Remember that student examining Ms. Ruddman, the three-hundred-pound epileptic, last month? She barely fits on the exam table anyway. She had run out of her seizure medicines, and the student went in alone to take her history. Suddenly, we heard a rattling sound in room two, followed by a crash that shook the floor! The nurse ran in and found that Ms. Ruddman was on the floor, having a grand mal seizure, and this terrified med student's head was caught clamped between her knees!"

This, of course, did little to lower Obie's anxiety level as he managed a nervous laugh.

"I'm Mark Kaufman, AR, and this is Jennifer Waters, JAR."

"Hi. I'm Obie Hardy, M-81."

"Just follow me into the rooms. I'll do the speculum exam; you will be able to see best from behind me. You can follow my bimanual exam, unless the patient objects."

"Okay." He followed Dr. Kaufman down the hallway to the first exam room. The patient's chart was in a pocket mounted on the door, and Dr. Kaufman lifted it out and leafed through the pages.

"The nurses will have gotten the vital signs and a UA already and charted the reason for the visit: follow-up, birth-control pills, vaginal discharge, etc."

Obie didn't wish to appear unknowledgeable, but couldn't assimilate the term "UA". "UA?" he queried.

"Urinalysis," answered Dr. Kaufman mechanically as he opened the door and stepped into the exam room. Obie followed, entering a new world of enlightenment. So far, his clinical experience had been limited to male military veterans, most of whom were middle-aged to elderly. Even his anatomy cadaver in first year had been male. Unclaimed bodies compiled the majority of cadavers, and such stiffs were predominately male. Also, all of his patients had needed psychiatric care for one reason or another. Now, seated on the exam table, was a young lady with a paper gown around her. She had shoulder-length brown hair and a few acne bumps, evidence of actively circulating female hormones. Her makeup partially concealed these dermal signals of bustling gonadal function. Smooth, shaven legs dangled from below the knee-length gown, her crossed ankles being the only clue that she may be a bit anxious.

Dr. Kaufman asked her some questions, verified her type of birth-control pill, and listened to her lungs, heart, and abdomen with his stethoscope. Obie was largely unaware of this activity, preoccupied with the anticipated urogenital exam. He was thinking of vagina, cervix, uterus, and ovaries. His pensive state dissipated when Dr. Kaufman opened the patient's gown, exposing her breasts. Obie was aware of his drive to stare at her bare bosom, his gaze drawn like a magnet to steel. He looked politely to the side, but was acutely aware of the nipple-tipped mounds in his peripheral vision.

"You can do the breast exam best with the arm laid up above the head," Dr. Kaufman narrated for Obie. "You use the pulps of three fingers and move in circular motions, covering the entire breast." Obie eagerly accepted this instruction as an invitation to observe Dr. Kaufman's breast exam and, coincidentally, the breasts. He noted Kaufman's mechanical exam technique, removing all sexual connotations from the act, except for the reflexive erection of the nipples, the autonomic response to manipulation. The breasts then disappeared under the gown again.

The nurse readied the patient for the pelvic exam, placing her feet in the stirrups and adjusting the table. Dr. Kaufman turned to the side and reached for some vinyl gloves, holding a pair out to Obie. He sat on the exam-table stool, adjusted the light, and pulled back the sheet covering the patient's pubic area. The vulva is a quite versatile structure, serving to house the urinary outlet, erogenous structures, protective fatty padding for the symphysis pubis bone, entrance for receiving the male phallus, and the outlet of the birth canal. It performs its functional roles, however, better than its aesthetic one. In this supine squatting type position on an exam table, the vulva resembles a shaggy, dried-up old potato. Dr. Kaufman moistened the stainless steel speculum with warm tap water and slid it into the potato, spreading the halves. He leaned to the side so Obie could see the cervix, a pink, glistening structure like a plum with a dimple in it. Obie watched the doctor scrape the cervix with a wooden blade and rub the end over a glass microscope slide for the Papinicolau stain—the PAP smear—and take two cotton swab samples — for microscopic examination and to test for gonorrhea. Dr. Kaufman removed the speculum, stood up between the patient's thighs, and put his right hand into her vagina, pushing down on her abdomen with his left.

"Use your non-dominant hand for the external abdominal examination and palpate the cervix, uterus, and ovaries with your dominant hand in the vagina. Okay, you can check her now."

Obie looked at the lady's face for a response to this direction. She was complacent. He stepped up between her thighs and placed his gloved right index and middle fingers into her vagina. It was well-lubricated already from the KY jelly Dr. Kaufman had applied, and his fingers slid in easily. It felt like he was reaching into a plastic bag of warm oatmeal, quite different from anatomic diagrams. He wriggled his fingers until he felt the plum of the cervix. Placing his left hand on her abdomen, he gingerly attempted to pin down the uterus and ovaries between his hand and his vaginal fingers. Only amorphous, warm oatmeal-like tissue could be perceived. His hands fumbled around for a while, but found no organs. Trying to emit a professional image, he abandoned his quest, pulled his inexperienced hand out of the oatmeal sack, and followed Dr. Kaufman from the room.

When Obie reported his fruitless exam, Dr. Kaufman told him that he wouldn't be able to find the ovaries on the first five to ten exams. Obie followed Dr. Kaufman from room to room, repeating the pelvic exam on birth-control-pill patients, pregnant women, irregular menstrual-cycle sufferers, and those harboring sexually transmitted diseases, STDs, the euphemism for VD. Soon he could distinguish the uterus but had not identified an ovary. He learned how to examine vaginal discharges for yeast and trichomonas infections with the microscope. Somehow, the vinyl gloves didn't convince him that he had not soiled his hands, and he stopped at every sink he passed to wash up.

At the end of the clinic, he had "examined" about fifteen women and had only palpated the uteri of those who were three or more months pregnant. He had yet to feel an ovary. Hands on exams were nothing like the anatomic diagrams he had studied. That night he reviewed his textbook, *A Guide to Physical Examination* by Barbara Bates, and performed imaginary exams, trying to improve his technique. Nevertheless, the following day he worked at the A. D. Williams clinic at MCV and was still unable to trap an ovary between his fingers. Was his grasp of anatomy misconceived? Did he not possess the skill or dexterity for such an exam? Were the authors of advice column letters in *Penthouse* more masterful than he, even after years of studying anatomy and biology?

Priscilla sensed Obie's despair when he came over for dinner. He explained his ineptness and even doubted his future in the field of medicine. She had dated Obie for over two years and was used to his moods, especially during the school year. Priscilla was a true southern belle from coastal North Carolina. Her features were soft, as well as her voice, and her words were never rushed. Her big brown eyes could always sooth Obie, who could gaze into them until his troubles were lost.

"Would it be helpful to practice on me?" she offered, with genuine sincerity.

"Well … maybe. I wouldn't be so rushed, like I was holding up the clinic." He hated himself for accepting her offer, especially since she had already allowed him to stab her arm twice while learning venipuncture. He had also practiced other parts of the physical exam on her over the past few months. She had endured the blinding halogen light of his ophthalmoscope beamed into her eye and the cold stainless steel bell of his stethoscope on her chest. Obie even violated her pet cat, Motley, by placing the base of his vibrating tuning fork on top of Motley's skull, sending her scurrying from the room, shaking her head. This abuse was more subtle than slapping Priscilla around, but he still felt the guilt afterward, knowing he had used someone who loved him. Well, he hadn't felt guilty about buzzing the cat.

Obie and Priscilla were close companions and, although maintaining separate residences, practically lived together. The enjoyed the same foods, music, and movies. Sex was infrequent, so much so that Obie often teased her, labeling her an "asexual". Theirs was not a lusty relationship.

So, Priscilla disrobed from the waist down while Obie washed his hands. While positioning her supine and flexed kneed on the bed, he appreciated the convenience of the exam tables with stirrups. Having moistened two of his right fingers with warm water, Obie slowly and gently inserted them into her vagina. This was a different feeling, no vinyl glove or KY, just flesh touching flesh. Her found her cervix easily and, by exerting pressure on her abdomen with his left hand, outlined the uterus. She tightened her abdominal muscles when he pressed on either side, just above the groin area, searching for an ovary. After three gropes, he felt a small nodule to the left of her uterus, and she flinched, "Oh!"

"I'm sorry," Obie responded. "That's the ovary!" He noted it was the size of a butter bean and rubbery. It was pinned between the fingers of his hands. He repositioned his hands onto her right side and, after two more probes, caught the right ovary between his fingers. Again, she flinched. "Is that painful?"

"No. It's just sore when you push down." He knew what it felt like to have a testicle squeezed and sympathized with her response. He withdrew his hands, having successfully completed his quest. Somehow, though, the accomplishment was vacuous. Instead of feeling pride and self-satisfaction with his acquired skill, he went to wash his hands, feeling ashamed. The wholesome bonding they enjoyed seemed a little frayed. Physical examination is such a cold objective process, not a warm mutual exchange of information; not a shared experience.

Obie drove home to his place to sleep that night, trying to escape the heavy feelings he was experiencing. He had made some excuse such as needing a textbook that was at home or an early clinic start the next day. He postulated that this sensation was one reason physicians didn't treat their own family members. By the next morning, the feeling had dissipated.

At the lecture room that morning, he was feeling a little confidence, knowing he had palpated an ovary. John Morgan approached him, beaming, "Hey, Obie. What's the difference between business and pleasure for a gynecologist?... A rubber glove!"

Obie laughed lightly, the levity smothered by the memory of last night's examination without a rubber glove.

After the morning lecture, Obie went to his assigned clinic in the A. D. Williams building. The OB-GYN residents staffing the clinic had the students take the patient history, write up the medical note, and examine the patient, with the resident reexamining the patient as the students finished. Obie saw only five patients, but felt more like he was contributing to their medical care than at the health department clinic. He learned how to question patients to obtain relevant information and how to write up the history and physical findings. There were many abbreviations used in OB-GYN medical histories that were important to learn: OBCP equals oral birth control pills; LMP equals last menstrual period; SVD equals spontaneous vaginal delivery; vaginal DC equals vaginal discharge; GC equals gonococcal (gonorrhea) infection; TAH equals transabdominal hysterectomy; BSO equals bilateral salpingo-opherectomy; PID equals pelvic inflammatory disease; and D&C equals dilation and curettage.

Mastering the shorthand acronyms was more complex than Obie had imagined. After his second A. D. Williams clinic day, he felt comfortable reading and writing this new language, until he arrived to work in the OB emergency room the next day. The first chart he attempted to read said, "20 yo BF G3P1A1 LMP=2-12-79 EDC=11-19-80

"6 wk S/P UTI c/o lower abd pain, urinary freq X 3d

"S/P SAb 1978. NKA

"Gravid BF in NAD

"Back- o CVAT

"Abd- FH=28, FHT=140, nontender, o UC

"Vag- long, closed

"IUP 29 WD/28 WS

"UTI."

He knew the basic abbreviations for "twenty-year-old black female" and "last menstrual period," as well as "NKA" for "no known allergies," and "NAD" for "no acute distress." He waited until the OB-GYN resident was not busy and asked for an interpretation. It was the third-year AR from the city clinic, Dr. Kaufman. He spoke in a matter-of-fact monotone.

"Okay. I see we still have to teach you studs how to read and write. Let's see ..." As he began reading from the chart, Obie looked on, and John peered over his shoulder, also poised to hear. "'Twenty-year-old black female, gravida-3,' which means this is her third pregnancy. 'Para-1' which means one prior birth. 'Abortus-1' meaning one miscarriage or abortion. 'Last menstrual period' began '2-12-79,' and 'estimated date of confinement,' which is her due date, of '11-19-80.' She is 'six weeks status—post-urinary tract infection' and 'complains of lower abdominal pain, urinary frequency for three days.' She is 'status—post-spontaneous abortion,' which is a miscarriage, in '1978.' 'No known allergies.'

"'Gravid,' or pregnant, 'black female in no acute distress.'

"'Back—no costovertebral angle tenderness.'

"'Abdomen—fundal height twenty-eight centimeters, fetal heart tones of 140 per minute, nontender, no uterine contractions.'

"'Vaginal—cervix long and closed,' which means no impeding

labor.

"'Intrauterine pregnancy, twenty-nine weeks by dates, twenty-eight weeks by size.'

"'Urinary tract infection.'"

Obie was fascinated by this translation, "Amazing!"

John grinned, teeth gleaming.

"Part of this is to cut down on the writing," explained Dr. Kaufman, "but, really, it's because doctors can't spell all these terms!"

Obie and John laughed understandingly. Obie wondered why his premed advisor had pushed him into taking Latin. Doctors sure used another language, but it was far from that used by Caesar.

"This your first time in 'the Pit'?"

"'The Pit'?" responded John.

"Yeah. That's what it's called. It has nothing to do with pitocin used in inductions of labor. It's because L&D is on the eleventh floor, West Hospital, and we are ground level of East Hospital. Labor patients have to go down to the basement to reach West Hospital, through the tunnels. Hence, we are down in the dungeon, 'The Pit.'"

Another doctor came through the door to the left of the front desk. He was tall with sandy blond hair, slightly receding hairline, and bright, sparkling blue eyes.

"This is Dr. Guthrie," gestured Kaufman. "He's the intern today."

"Hi!" Dr. Guthrie said and turned to Dr. Kaufman. "This one's got Trichomonas. Since metronidazole is possibly teratogenic, we can't treat her until late third trimester or after delivery. I'll recommend a Betadine douche once for palliative therapy."

"Fine," he responded, taking the yellow hieroglyphic patient chart and scanning Dr. Guthrie's note.

"Sounds like the A. D. Williams Clinic," John told Obie.

"Well, yeah," responded Kaufman. "This is 'Turf City.' Any woman presenting to the MCV-ER is asked when their last menstrual period was. If it's four weeks or more past, they're turfed to 'The Pit'. But, if they're under eighteen, they can be turfed to the pediatric ER. So, regardless of what their medical problem is, like a heart attack or the intestinal flu, they end up in 'The Pit.'"

"So, you don't just see pregnant women in the OB ER?" queried John.

"That's right! Anything that has to do with females can end up here. We have an asthmatic in the back getting IV meds. She'll probably be discharged in three or four hours. You can accompany Dr. Guthrie seeing patients, but I'd rather you not see patients alone yet."

As his words ended, there was a brief silence before the metal-clad, double swinging doors in front of the desk burst open. There was a young black woman with an enormously bulging abdomen waddling in. Her eyes were frightened, her face glistening with sweat, and she held her abdomen with her left hand. A nurse appeared from nowhere and assisted her to a stretcher while interrogating her.

"How many times have you been pregnant?"

"… Third time …"

"How many babies have you had?"

"Two."

"Are you having contractions?"

"Yes … Oh, Jesus!" she screamed, tensing up her body and gripping tightly the side rails of the stretcher.

"Don't hold your breath! Keep breathing, in and out!" ordered the nurse. "In and out. Breathe!"

Dr. Kaufman went to the bedside and picked up a dirty, white envelope the woman had been carrying. As he glanced over its contents, Dr. Guthrie approached the group.

"Bainbridge Clinic," read Dr. Kaufman. "EDC 8-15-79; blood type O-positive; borderline anemic."

"About forty-five seconds," reported the nurse. "When did your pains start?" she continued.

"About three hours ago," she reported between deep breaths. "Any gush of water or blood?"

"No."

There was a snapping sound as Dr. Guthrie pulled a rubber glove onto his right hand. The nurse was helping the woman remove her panties as she closed the curtain around the stretcher. Obie and John were still standing at the desk, amazed by the flurry of activity.

"Six centimeters, 90 percent, zero to minus one," called out Guthrie from behind the curtain.

"Okay, let's get her up there," answered Dr. Kaufman. "Where are the studs? You still here, studs?"

Obie and John exchanged glances, realizing they were being beckoned. Medical students frequently have their title reduced to *stud*. This is supposedly an affectionate nickname, although blatantly sexist. M-81s soon discovered, however, that when addressed as "studs", they were expected to perform as a workhorse, not the prized breeder the name implied.

"Get over here!" They scampered behind the drape to the patient's bedside. "Can you start an IV?"

"Sure!" chirped John, rocking on his feet, side to side, in eager anticipation.

"The IV tray is behind the desk," directed Kaufman, and John leaped into action. The nurse placed a bedpan under the patient and, when full, handed it to Obie.

"Check a dipstick urine. The strips are in the back room by the microscope," ordered Kaufman. Obie carried the urine through the swinging doors and saw a counter on the right. The wall was stained with splatters of blood and yellow-brown fluid splashes around the countertop. A microscope and centrifuge sat on the counter with a canister of urine dipsticks. Obie took out a test strip and plunged it into the urine, pulling it back out to compare its colored squares to those on the canister label. As he was deciphering the puzzle of colored squares, Dr. Guthrie burst through the doors, holding three tubes of blood. He pulled the lavender cap off of one tube and stuck the end of a glass capillary tube into the blood. After plugging the end with gum in a small tray on the counter, he placed it in the centrifuge and switched it on.

"The urine show anything?" he asked.

"Ah ... " Obie hesitated, "pH is 6.5, ... specific gravity 1.015, and ... protein is trace."

"Good!" he said as he wrote on the patient's clipboard, the increasing roar of the centrifuge muffling his words. "We'll call up the 'crit!"

Obie followed him back out the doors and Kaufman and John were turning the patient's stretcher to roll her out of the ER, IV hanging on the attached pole.

"Take her up!" said Kaufman, motioning to John and Dr. Guthrie. As they rolled her out of the ER, Dr. Kaufman stepped over to the front desk and called labor and delivery, or L&D. "We just sent up a twenty-seven-year-old black female, G3P2, at term, in active labor; six centimeters, 90 percent. Her name is Harris. Dr. Guthrie's bringing her up. My guess is 3250."

Obie was impressed. This entire episode took about ten minutes. As Dr. Kaufman hung up, there was a click and ding from the back room and a whining as the centrifuge began to slow down.

"You ever read a 'crit?" asked Kaufman.

"No," replied Obie, following him to the centrifuge. Dr. Kaufman removed the capillary tube and place it on a diagonal grid card taped to the counter. He showed Obie how to line up the bottom, top, and red cell layers.

"Thirty-four," he read. "Call that up to L&D." Obie obeyed. The flurry of events had his mind spinning, trying to absorb the patient management routine that had just transpired.

"What's 3250?" asked Obie.

"3250 grams. My estimate of the fetal weight."

"How did you estimate that?"

"It's just a guess. You feel the fetal size during Leopold's and give it a rough estimate. Average is 3500 grams, seven and a half pounds. This one's a little below average."

Obie sensed it was like when a fisherman reports he caught a "six-pound bass." Most fishermen don't carry scales on their boats, and the fish weight that they report is accepted by peers. Also, fishermen know that a fish loses weight when removed from the water, so that when the boat returns to the dock, the fish weighs five and a half pounds. The real weight, therefore, is the estimated six pounds, since that was the "wet weight". Obie wondered if an infant's true weight is its "wet weight", or predelivery estimate. He imagined a mother saying, "Yeah, … he weighed in at seven pounds but his 'wet weight' before I squeezed him through my birth canal was seven and a half!"

John didn't return for about an hour. He walked through the door, face aglow. "Well, Obie, I got my first delivery!" he said, holding out his hands like one would hold a basketball, and then pulling them toward himself, simulating the birth process. "A girl—3,180 grams!"

"3250, wet weight," thought Obie to himself, smiling.

"I guess the next one's yours. It was great!" Obie was excited about the thought of delivering a baby, but also terrified, having been taught about so many of the complications. There would not be time to stop and read up on any problem that might arise. Anyway, his turn didn't come that day. The remainder of the shift was much like the Health Department clinic: UTIs, VD, yeast infections, morning sickness, and constipation—anticlimactic.

After several days, the students were permitted to see patients alone and present their assessments to the OB residents. This helped bolster Obie's confidence some in managing OB-GYN cases. The residents would recheck pertinent findings and write the required prescriptions.

One afternoon in the Pit, Obie entered an exam room to see a patient. Usually, the nurse already had the patient in a hospital gown with a sheet draped over her legs in preparation for an examination. Obie introduced himself as a student doctor and saw before him a lovely, slender female brunette with brown eyes and no clothing. She sat on the exam table holding a sheet up over her bosom. Her dark eyes seemed to gaze at him. He realized she didn't have on an exam gown and tried to ignore her smooth, bare shoulders.

"I ... er ... see ... from your chart, ... that you've been having some discharge," stumbled Obie as he looked in the cabinet under the exam table for a gown or at least another sheet. Having stooped down in his search, he became aware of her clean-shaven legs at his eye level.

"Yes," she answered. Obie stood up quickly and turned to the shelves behind him, continuing his nervous search.

"Well ... ah ... when did it start?"

"About two days ago," answered the lips under those deep, rich eyes. Obie felt a radiance, a sexuality, glowing from this young woman. His search for a garment had been as unproductive as his uneasiness with the situation. Trying to maintain his professionalism, he continued his medical history, asking about urinary and menstrual symptoms.

"Well, let's see what we can find out," said Obie, laying aside the clipboard. He listened to her lungs with his stethoscope between her shoulder blades and tapped over her kidneys with his fist. The crease along her spine flowed down to her waist, stopping just short of the cleavage between her buttocks, where her sacral dimples added a pleasant accent to her shape. "Ah ... could you lay back, please?"

The single sheet posed a problem for completing the non-gynecologic examination. To access the heart or abdomen, the drape would have to be lowered, exposing her breasts, or raised, exposing her pubic area. Without waiting for directions, she laid back and lowered the sheet, uncovering two perfect appearing breast mounds. Unconsciously, Obie held his breath as he carefully placed his stethoscope beside her left breast, attempting to auscultate her heart. The pulsating cardiac sounds were partially drowned out by his own heartbeat pounding in his head. He also noticed a pulsation in his lower stomach, just below his waist, causing a swelling in his crotch. Stepping back from the patient, he felt his erection pressing against his khakis. He turned and reached for the clipboard, holding it in front of himself to hide his growing sexual arousal.

"Well … I'm … ah, going to get the nurse … so we can do the female check … I'll be back in a minute." Obie headed for the door, still shielding himself with the clipboard as he stepped out of the room.

"Are you ready to do the pelvic?" asked the nurse, seeing Obie emerge from the room.

"Oh … er … yes," answered Obie, continuing his shield as she walked past him into the room. As the door was closing behind her, he heard her voice.

"Oh. You can't be examined like that! I'll get you a gown." A moment later, the door reopened. "We're out of gowns in that room. I'll get some more. We'll be ready in a few minutes," she reported as she walked past Obie. She briefly looked back over her shoulder, an inquisitive look that Obie tried not to notice. He hoped she didn't suspect anything out of the ordinary. Had she noticed him covering his crotch or, even worse, what he was trying to hide? Was she suspicious that he had acted unprofessionally or taken liberties with this patient? He had never been physically aroused by a patient before, and this involuntary reaction left him questioning his medical objectivity. Could he be perverted?

John approached him later that afternoon with his ever-present grin. "Obie, did you hear the one about the patient with a lisp?"

"No."

"The doctor was examining a well-endowed lady. He was listening to her lungs, and her gown fell off as he put his stethoscope on her back. 'Big breaths,' he said.

"'Why thankth you, docthor,' she said."

Medical College of Virginia, West Hospital

Chapter 4
L&D

The main hospital of the MCV complex was West Hospital. The floor plan was shaped like a cross, with three elevators and a stairway encircling the hub of the cross. Most floors had a circular desk station in the center of the hub where the ward clerk was stationed. The eleventh floor was missing the desk station, since it housed operating rooms and L&D. L&D filled the south wing of West-11. Obie looked around the hub as he stepped off the elevator, awed by the shining, dark gray, rock-patterned floor. He walked through the double, swinging, stainless-steel-door entrance to L&D, hoping there would be coffee there to perk up the evening fog feeling in his head. It seemed ironic that Labor Day was his first day in L&D. He walked slowly down the hall, looking about for a clue as to where to report in. A nurse in blue-gray surgical scrubs stepped into the hall from a door to the left side.

"Hey! Don't step across the red line!" she ordered him. Obie looked down and saw that his feet were already across the red line, and he quickly retreated. "You have to be in scrubs to enter the labor and delivery areas," she continued as she crossed the hall to his right. "You can change in the residents' room to your left. Scrubs, masks, and shoe covers are here." She pointed to the right to a large rack of surgical scrubs and boxes of shoe covers and masks. Obie thanked her and collected a set of surgical wear.

The residents' room was small, containing a military-style, wooden bunk bed, a desk with a lamp, a metal locker, several chairs, and a blackboard on the wall beside the bunks. Walter Ferguson, another stud on OB rotation, was tying his scrub pants as Obie entered.

"Hey, Obie," he greeted. He was a soft-spoken, gentle person. Even his thin, brunette mustache appeared soft. "Did you bike in today?"

"Yeah, this morning. The sunrise was pretty crossing over I-95, and not much traffic at 5:30 a.m."

John Morgan came through the door behind Obie, teeth bright as a sunrise, eyes sparkling, and holding a steaming styrofoam cup. He looked like a real doctor, wearing scrubs instead of the student's standard short white coat.

"Obie! Good evening!"

"Evening," replied Obie, intentionally skipping the "good" adjective. He stared enviously at his coffee, certain that no one was that cheerful and perky after being at work twelve hours without having caffeine.

"There's coffee across the hall in the nurses' station."

The senior attending resident, AR, in charge of L&D was Peggy Johnson. She was above-average in height with thick, dark brown hair to just below her shoulders. Her complexion was dark, and, although she appeared thirtyish, she portrayed a seasoned maturity. Jennifer Waters was the JAR on duty. Dr. Johnson was seated on the bunk bed in the residents' room when Obie returned with his coffee, wearing his scrub suit. John and Walter were engrossed in tying suture threads that were sewn into the fabric of the cushion of a chair.

"Always keep the tie with the needle attached in the same hand," instructed Dr. Johnson. "Cross the other tie over the needle tie first. Tie. Then cross under it, alternating with each throw of the knot."

Obie watched, wondering what use these surgical ties would be to medical students in the delivery room. Would a medical student help in suturing during a C-section?

"Episiotomies are a bear to learn suturing on, but it's a very forgiving area. The scars never show."

Dr. Waters stepped halfway in the doorway and said, "Peggy, the next PGE suppository is due now. I think she's starting. She's having some cramps now."

Dr. Johnson left the room. Obie recalled that prostaglandin E, PGE, induced labor and was used for "therapeutic" abortions, eliminating the need for surgical evacuation of the products of conception. There was, however, a problem with such a naturally induced abortion.

"The problem with the prostaglandin abortions is that aborted fetus is often born alive," explained Dr. Waters. "The rule is, only the senior residents can give the suppositories, so that the life/death resuscitation decision rests on them."

John Morgan followed Dr. Waters into the labor room, where a female patient was struggling with nature's chore. When John returned, he walked over to the white plastic relief chart in the wall and spread open two fingers. When he matched his finger span with a raised circle on the chart, he reported, "Five centimeters. She's halfway there."

Obie, realizing an educational value of the chart, compared his finger spans to the different cervical dilation widths. This would certainly be a different type of pelvic exam, hopefully easier to learn than the bimanual exam. His practice model, Priscilla, would take at least nine months to be useful in learning this skill.

Dr. Waters invited the students into the labor room, where a black woman was being monitored. The doppler fetal monitor beat a rapid rhythm, almost like a slow drum roll. She explained that each student should follow a patient's labor and then assist with that patient's delivery. Seeing the monitor strips of uterine contraction patterns, fetal heart rates, and the graph of dilation and station led Obie to believe that childbirth was an almost mathematically chartable biological process. Dr. Waters continued orienting them to the delivery rooms and adjoining surgical scrub rooms. The C-sections were usually done across the hall in the larger rooms. As they walked through the surgical suite, something in the corner moved, catching the students' attentions. It was a fetus, the size of a Barbie doll. The umbilical cord was severed, and dark blood was oozing out. The eyelids were fused closed, and the infant would periodically gasp as if trying to breathe.

"Just ignore that," continued Dr. Waters. "The prostaglandin abortions often are alive for a short period. When the eyelids haven't separated, the lungs are too underdeveloped to sustain life. The residents hide them from the patients, because it's too traumatic for them to see the fetus moving. Let's go on." She led the group back into the hall. Obie lagged behind briefly, his eyes fixed on this living organism, abandoned and slowly dying from lack of oxygen, exposure, and blood loss. The gasping actions reminded him of a fish out of water, lying on the ground, making breathing movements in attempts to draw oxygen in through its gills. He had to ignore his most natural instinct to help other beings, relieve suffering. This was indeed a cold and inhospitable world. He turned and walked out into the hall where he could hear Dr. Johnson's voice behind the closed door to the labor room across the hall. No doubt she was soothing the woman who had just suffered through the physical and emotional trauma of an abortion. Suddenly, there was a squeaking sound, and Obie looked back at the door hiding the fetus, sensing the noise was a high-pitched, mouse-like cry for help. His heart skipped a beat, until he turned away and saw the residents' room door closing, its hinges squeaking.

Obie felt secure in the residents' room, but emerged at intervals to survey the progress of the patients in labor and look for new patients to follow. John was determined to do the delivery on the present patient. Obie began following a young Caucasian girl in labor, Alice King. It was her first pregnancy, a primagravida, and for the next six hours, her labor graphs remained flat lines. Obie had checked her cervix after Dr. Johnson every two hours, but she remained four to five centimeters dilated. Dr. Johnson ordered a pelvis X-ray to determine if her pelvis was of adequate size to deliver vaginally. The students crowded around the X-ray view box in the residents' room as Dr. Johnson measured the diagonal conjugate, interspinous, and anterioposterior diameter of the pelvic outlet. She explained that the pelvic inlet is 1.5 centimeters less than the diagonal conjugate and must be ten centimeters or more for a vaginal delivery. Ms. King had a diagonal conjugate of ten centimeters, and therefore a contracted pelvis. She recommended a C-section.

Obie observed the bustling activity preparing for a C-section. The anesthetist questioned the patient as Dr. Johnson and Dr. Waters scrubbed for surgery. The pediatrician arrived as the nurses prepared the OR, unwrapping instrument packs and stocking the instrument table with betadine and gauze sponges. Alice King was rolled into the OR, placed on the operating table, and had the blue surgical drapes positioned as a nurse scrubbed her bulging abdomen with the brown antiseptic prep. The anesthetist was placing the heart electrodes on her chest and preparing several syringes of medicines, arranging them on his table like an assortment of spices on a rack. Dr. Johnson looked to the pediatrician and to the anesthetist, getting verbal affirmations of readiness. The anesthetist held the mask over the patient's mouth and nose and gave the IV bolus of Sodium Pentathol. Within seconds, he reported, "She's ready."

Dr. Johnson made a quick sweeping transverse incision as the nurse called out, "Two thirty-four a.m." Dr. Waters blotted away the bleeding as Dr. Johnson continued to slice into the uterus, but now much more delicately. "Forty-five seconds," reported the nurse. Suddenly, Dr. Johnson's hands plunged into the surgical wound, disappearing past her wrists. A clear fluid with trickles of blood poured over the edges of the wound as Dr. Waters suctioned copiously. A hair-covered ball appeared in the wound as the nurse chanted, "One minute." The doctors fumbled with the infant's limbs and isolated the umbilical cord. Dr. Waters clamped it and cut it free as Dr. Johnson turned and handed the grayish infant to the pediatrician. It was smeared with whitish, cream-cheese-like substance and dripping with watery and bloody fluid. "One minute, twenty seconds," announced the nurse.

Walter Ferguson was standing with Obie, watching the miraculous procedure. "It's like a rocket-launch countdown," he remarked.

"Why are they so pressured by time?" asked Obie.

"I guess so the anesthesia doesn't suppress the baby's respirations." Obie noticed that the pediatrician was still stimulating a fairly limp infant, who was just beginning to make some gasps for air. He did appear sedated some.

"Apgar at one minute is seven," announced the pediatrician. It was a two-ring circus—newborn resuscitation to the left and placenta removal with uterine closure to the right. Closing the womb was infinitely more tedious than opening; understandably, since a mass of muscle tissue the size of a tangerine had been spread out to coat the surface of a mass the size of a basketball. It is wondrous how an organ stretched to that extent could rhythmically contract with enough force to squeeze the fetal payload through the birth canal.

Alice King struggled to regain wakefulness in the recovery room. She opened her eyes, feeling dizzy and seeing hazy lights. There was a nauseating feeling compounding the intolerable aching in her lower abdomen that felt even worse than the uterine contractions. As through a tunnel, she heard a voice calling, "Ms.

King? Are you awake?"

She tried to speak, but her throat was swollen, and she couldn't even hear her own hoarse whisper as she mouthed, "Yes." Her eyes fixed on a red-and-white sign beside the stretcher.

"Ms. King? ...You had a baby boy! What are you going to name him?"

The words on the sign began to come into focus, growing clearer, as if a prophetic message. She read aloud, *"No ... Smo ... King.* Nosmo King!" Comforted that her son had been delivered, named, and her labor over, her eyes closed, and she drifted back into a restful slumber.

Obie's second night in L&D held promise of his first hands-on delivery. He was following Ruby Taylor, currently in labor with her fourth child. Other than being overweight, her only medical problem was asthma. She had paroxysmal spells of coughing that disrupted the fetal-monitor tracings tremendously, interrupting the labor graph with senseless outbursts of scribbling. Obie knew that orderly, textbook, graph of labor did not exist. In reality, biological systems are predictably unpredictable, and labor can take from four to forty-eight hours and still be viewed as normal. Ruby Taylor's labor was, therefore, not exceptional. With such scribbled tracings, her course was evaluated only by serial pelvic checks, attempted to be done between coughing fits. Obie's inexperienced hand needed extra time to ascertain the anatomy and constitution of the cervix, especially since his exams were always interrupted by coughing. Dr. Johnson was attending this patient and appeared slightly concerned, pondering the possible problems the coughing could cause with delivery.

Ruby Taylor became suddenly agitated and restless, churning her arms and legs on the gurney. Dr. Johnson quickly came to the bedside and performed a cervical check. Clear water with the musty smell of amniotic fluid gushed from the vagina as she felt for the cervix.

"She's complete and plus-one!" she exclaimed. "Let's get her to the delivery room." Turning to Obie as she snapped the glove off her hand, "Better get scrubbed if you want this delivery!"

Obie's mind was racing with the excitement of his first delivery, but his body seemed to move in slow motion. He masked his face and began the seven-minute surgical scrub, trying to duplicate the procedure from the videotape he had been shown in orientation. He watched the second hand on the clock as he probed the dirt from under his fingernails. Dr. Johnson attacked the scrub sink bedside him, wet her hands and forearms, splashed the light brown liquid soap on them—barely enough to foam, and rinsed off. She shoved her hip into the swinging door to the delivery room, calling to Obie, "You'd better come on!"

Obie glanced at the clock. *Five and a half more minutes*, he thought as he began scrubbing the side of each digit. He heard Ruby Taylor groan and scream in the next room, followed by a bout of coughing. *Five more minutes.* He looked through the door window as Dr. Johnson was arranging the delivery table and coated the woman's perineum with Betadine solution. *Four more minutes.* More coughing ensued, and Dr. Johnson focused her attention on Ruby Taylor's vagina, spotlighted by the ceiling-mounted light. Obie could not see for the woman's draped leg was blocking the view. *Three minutes.* Obie scrubbed the surfaces of his forearms, front, back, and sides, and then repeated the detailed scrubbing of his hands and fingers. His skin tingled from the rough surface of the sponge. *Two and a half minutes.* More coughing was heard from the delivery room. This spell was interrupted by the patient pausing to catch her breath and cry out in pain. *Two minutes.* Obie remembered that he had heard of the five-minute scrub but that the sterile conditions were maximized by the seven-minute scrub. He still couldn't see Dr. Johnson's hands for the draped leg. *One minute!* He heard the coughing intensify as he rapidly passed the sponge over his forearms again and rinsed off his hands, holding them up so that the water ran off his elbows. He pushed through the door and turned to see Dr. Johnson holding a plump male infant and reaching for a Kelly clamp for the umbilical cord.

"I said to come on," she said to Obie.

"I know," he responded. "I hadn't finished the seven-minute scrub," he explained, realizing how ridiculous that sounded.

"Well," she continued, "there're scrubs and there're scrubs. You have to take care of the patient even if it means a twenty-second scrub. Mother Nature waits for no one."

Thus went Obie's second night in L&D, strike two. John had done three deliveries already. Obie wondered when he would ever experience delivering a baby. He had ridden with the county rescue squad his senior year in college. The squad members prided themselves on deliveries, one even boasted to have delivered twins. They joked about slowing the ambulance down and taking the bumpy back streets to the hospital when a new member had an opportunity for his first delivery. Even city taxi drivers had done deliveries. Obie approached his third night at bat with continued anxiety.

Lawanda Richardson was his next labor patient, a veteran of two previous births. Dr. Jennifer Waters was to do the delivery or, hopefully, guide Obie through his first delivery. Obie graphed out her labor course well, and she advanced to completely dilated over six hours, ready for the delivery room.

Dr. Waters talked to Obie while he nervously scrubbed, trying to dispel his anxiety. Obie cut short his scrub at five minutes, taking no chances. He stood at Dr. Waters's side as she surveyed the sterile table, readying the clamps and the local anesthetic and arranging the scissors: straight for episiotomy, curved for sutures. The nurses positioned Ms. Richardson on the delivery table in the lithotomy position, the position one would be in if their rocking chair tipped over backward. Her wrists were belted in place with leather straps, positioned to grasp the stainless steel handgrips on each side. If she were dressed in a helmet and bulky white flight suit instead of linen-draped nudity, she would be positioned as a spread-legged astronaut gazing skyward, awaiting lift-off. The countdown continued …

"This will be cold on your bottom," announced Dr. Waters as she poured the iodine solution over the stargazer's crotch and inner thighs. Once the surgical green drapes were in place over her legs and abdomen, her personage had been reduced to about one square foot of brown-tinted skin. A contraction ensued, spreading the labia to expose the hairy, wet bulge of a fetal head. Dr. Waters pressed her gloved hand over Obie's and pressed it against the head. "About this much pressure should be applied to the head to prevent it from suddenly 'popping' out." Her hand felt steady and sure. His felt like it was trembling rapidly, but, even as he looked closely at it, he could not see it shaking.

As Obie held his hand on the baby's head, the contraction abated, and the head retracted into the vagina. Dr. Waters then injected anesthetic into the perineum below the vagina and, upon the next contraction, cut the median episiotomy. She then held a sterile towel against the patient's rectum.

"The Ritgen maneuver helps pull the head up and out, under the pubic symphysis," she explained as she positioned Obie's hand on the towel. The contraction waned, Dr. Waters dropped the towel into the non-sterile world below and handed Obie a new one for the next contraction. The lull seemed like slow motion as the staff anticipated another contraction. Obie felt the trembling subside somewhat.

Ms. Richardson began a strained grunt, and the head bulged out as Obie applied digital counter-pressure. This time it came further, and he could feel it inch forward when he pushed his other, Ritgen hand upward on the towel. Suddenly, the head was out, facing down but turning to the mother's right. Dr. Waters quickly checked the neck and discovered the rubbery umbilical cord, which she pulled over the baby's head, announcing "Nuchal cord times one." She coached Obie, "Okay, pull downward to deliver the anterior shoulder."

Obie was amazed at how forceful she urged him to pull. The shoulder slid out, and Obie began pulling upward to guide out the posterior shoulder. The whole baby slipped out suddenly, following the shoulder, and Obie squatted down to get both hands under the wet, slippery infant. He saw Dr. Waters reflexively reaching out to catch the child, and, when he had a secure grip, he looked up and saw the panic in her eyes. Apparently, she had envisioned the child falling to the floor or even bouncing up and down by the rubbery umbilical cord, like a paddle-ball toy. She placed the Kelly clamps on the cord, cut it, and guided Obie to the incubator area to clean the baby.

"It's a boy!" she announced to Ms. Richardson, who sighed in relief and pleasure. She suctioned his mouth and rubbed him with a towel, initiating the first cry of a new life. "Apgar eight," she reported as she pinched the umbilical cord to count a pulse. "Taking off one for some peripheral cyanosis and one for tone." Obie still felt the fine tremor in his arms and a weakness, much like after lifting weights.

Obie was still feeling weak when he sat on the stool to complete suturing the episiotomy that Dr. Waters had begun repairing. He marveled that Ms. Richardson reported no discomfort from the wound or the stitching. Now the knot-tying practice in the residents' room proved useful.

"Don't ever scare me like that again," said Dr. Waters sternly, after mother and child were sent to recovery.

"I wasn't going to drop him," Obie explained. "I felt him slipping, so I just reached underneath him so I wouldn't jerk his neck or arm." He realized how spastic he must have looked.

"All right. Since you did the delivery, you write the delivery note." With direction from Dr. Waters, Obie produced his first delivery note:

Procedure: SVD - Med Episiotomy & Repair
Anesth: 1% lidoc local
Findings: TBLMI; Apgars 8-9-10
Complications: 2o tear perineum; Nuchal cord X 1
Est Blood Loss: 200 cc
Operators: Obie Hardy - M81

Jennifer Waters, MD - JAR

Obie was relieved now that he had done a delivery, but felt no euphoria that he had expected from bringing a child into the world. Trying to remember what to do, anticipating complications, relinquishing control over the process to the forces of nature, and reducing the experience to a less than thirty-word note brought the miracle of life to view under the light of medicine. It was a hard, impersonal reality accented by an anxious trembling that left Obie relieved and exhausted.

Priscilla met Obie for lunch the following day.

"Did you get to do a delivery yet?" she asked excitedly.

"Yeah, I did."

"Well, …boy or girl?"

"Ah, … a boy. Yes, it was a boy," remembering his "TBLMI," term birth live male infant, note. "It was pretty exciting. But, man, was I nervous!"

"Well, what did he weigh?"

Obie realized he didn't know the baby's weight, length, or name. The memory of fumbling the babe as it slipped out, however, was still quite vivid. He had forgotten to guess the wet weight and could hardly remember the Apgars. "I don't know," he answered, "… but it almost got away!"

Later, in the Pit, a short lady obviously late in her pregnancy approached the registration desk. She was white and not particularly clean, with worn clothing and tan, shoulder-length hair. Her vocabulary was limited as she explained her visit.

"I got 'dis rats between my legs and didn't know what to tic dat won't hurt de little baby."

Dr. Kaufman examined her with Obie, who was aghast that she had a wet, shiny, raw rash over her inner thighs and crotch area. It was obviously as painful as a bad sunburn or scalding. The compressed bladder had apparently been leaking urine over the area. The odor was strong, pungent, and musty. This condition has obviously been incubating for days or weeks. Her fetal heart rate was fine, and fetal movements could be felt. Dr. Kaufman dispensed the antifungal cream from the ER stock, instead of handing her a prescription, as per usual protocol.

After she left, Dr. Kaufman elaborated, "She's from Oregon Hill."

"Oregon Hill?" responded Obie.

"It's a slum-like area below the fan, by Hollywood Cemetery. She couldn't have been able to fill the prescription, and I even wonder about her bathing facilities."

"The Pit" was on the ground floor of East Hospital, or E. G. Williams. In bygone days of racial segregation, E. G. Williams was the black or colored hospital of MCV. Now, the post-partum ward was on the third floor. The ward on East 3, known as E3, was open like the VA hospital wards, divided into four sections, with a partial wall separating them. The M-81s would round on the new mothers each day after a performed delivery. The patients stayed until the third post-partum day routinely. The chart rack was a round, rolling table with the charts in a slotted carrousel on top. The carrousel turned like a lazy Susan, with the charts held like books in the slots. The protocol was to check the uterus, lungs, and leg veins daily and note the temperature and blood pressure. On the third day, a visual check of the genitals for healing and episiotomy stitches was done. The chart rack rolled from one bed to the next. Obie couldn't help feeling like the large, open ward was like a warehouse or factory, and that the medical team rolled along the assembly line. A rubber-inked stamp was used to punch off the post-partum note format, helping to complete the assembly-line image.

Obie managed five more deliveries over the next three weeks, in L&D every third night. Morning rounds always followed the twenty-fourth hour of the thirty-six-hour call day: the day clinic shift, the night L&D, and the following day clinic. Even young, eager M-81 studs felt the drain of the work hours. Obie was making E3 rounds on his patients alone, stamping the chart progress notes, and filling in the blanks with the "Post-partum Day # ___" and "Temp ___ BP _____". At six a.m., the patients were usually sleeping and frequently had to be awakened. Obie stopped beside the next bed, opening the chart and stamping it. The brunette, new mother was soundly sleeping, and Obie thought how peaceful she looked. She must have been tired from her ordeal and would need this sleep now, especially with a new infant. She was curled up to the right side of the bed, and Obie noticed the whole left side of her bed was vacant. He nudged her and she just sighed softly. He nudged again.

"Just a few more minutes," she begged quietly. He wondered, if he waited a few more minutes, he too would be asleep. He felt drawn to the empty half of her bed, it seemed to grow closer to him. His eyes became more blurry, even with a few ineffective cleansing blinks. His lids closed, and he was asleep.

Obie sleepily opened his eyes and noted the darkened room. How long had he been asleep? Well, he had been making rounds … What? He couldn't be in the brunette's bed! He was on the left side of the bed and felt the warmth of another body against his side. This could be the end of medical school. This was atrocious! He lay frozen, still, afraid a movement would announce his folly. He couldn't make out the details of the room in the dark, but it didn't look exactly like the E3 ward. But he had never seen the ward from a patient's bed! He had to do something. He looked at his bedmate's head, turned away from him. He reached out and gently turned her head toward him. In the dim light he thought she was familiar.

"Are you all right, honey?" asked the sleepy voice of Priscilla.

Obie was scared to move, but relieved. He was in bed with Priscilla!

"Uh-huh. Just had a dream."

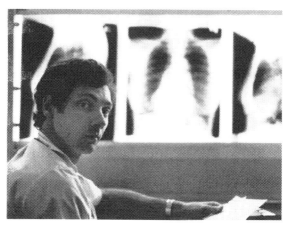

Hardy, M-81, at X-ray rounds

Chapter 5
North 7 Medicine

In mid-October, Richmond was vibrant with the flavor of the season changing from hazy, humid summer to autumn. The warehouses south of the river exuded the heady smell of ripe, cured tobacco. The aroma was intoxicating, inducing lightheadedness if inhaled for sustained periods. The oak and maple trees were gold and orange colored, with their fallen leaves sprinkling color over the usually drab streets and sidewalks. Mornings were cool and dew-filled or even laced with frost. The third-year medical students were also changing climates to new clinical rotations. Obie was beginning Internal Medicine, which was heralded as the most cerebral of the clinical fields. After all, it is called "Medical" School, the practice of "medicine," with the goal of receiving an MD, a doctorate degree in "medicine." Another season, another rotation, and … another hospital.

North Hospital was northeast of MCV West Hospital and housed the oncology clinic and radiation therapy in its lower levels. The top floor, North 8, was allocated to alcohol detoxification and rehabilitation. Obie was to report to the seventh floor, North 7, to begin his medicine rotation in general internal medicine. Walter Ferguson was the other student assigned to this outpost. The residents' room was in the corner of the south end of the floor. The windows looked out over Interstate 95 to Church Hill and up to the North End of Richmond. The crisp blue autumn sky seemed very close when viewed from seven stories above the city streets.

Both Obie and Walter had their pockets stuffed with pens, pen lights, Snelling vision cards, and a spiral-bound copy of *Washington Manual of Medical Therapeutics*, as well as their black bags of medical diagnostic tools. The three residents had been on this service for a week already, but joined the students in awaiting the arrival of the new attending. The attending doctor walked in and introduced himself.

"Hi. I'm Dr. George Whitehall, this month's attending." He was probably mid-forties in age, with short, lightly gray-peppered brown hair. His hair was slightly awry, and his black horn-rimmed glasses were visibly smudged. "I'm an Endocrinologist, currently involved in a research project. All faculty members rotate as attendings two months each year. It's a good experience and helps keep me current in clinical medicine."

He seemed pleasant enough. Obie wondered what research project Dr. Whitehall was involved in—maybe pancreas transplants, possibly the future "cure" for diabetes. It must certainly be more high tech than Obie's second-year summer research project. Dr. Paul Felton, the JAR, led the group on rounds on the eighteen patients, giving a brief clinical summary at each bedside but referring questions to the appropriate intern managing each case. Since the students were only expected to workup new admissions, Obie was able to meet Priscilla for lunch.

The hot dog vendor carts on the street corners around MCV provided an adequate fast lunch. Obie referred to such a meal as grabbing "a dog on the street." He and Priscilla ate the foil-wrapped "dogs" while sitting in the garden area beside the education building, Sanger Hall.

"I'm on call tomorrow night," he announced.

"Okay. Who's on the rotation with you?"

"Ferg … It shouldn't be too high-powered," he replied, trying to make the intensity of internal medicine seem less. He paused, pensive, realizing that medicine would not be much less stressful just because easygoing Walter Ferguson was on the rotation.

"So, when can I see you?"

"Well, I'll probably get an admission today and have to do a presentation tomorrow. I'll need to prepare that tonight, take call tomorrow night, and sleep the next night. How about Thursday?"

"Well," she sighed, "I guess I can clean the apartment some this week, maybe wash some clothes."

"I'm sorry. I'm just anxious about this rotation. It's one-fourth of our entire clinical year. I'll call you tonight, okay?"

"All right, but Thursday better mean an Italian dinner."

"Okay. The Bella Italia, Thursday."

By the next morning's rounds, Walter Ferguson had a neatly prepared, four-and-a-half-page hand-written workup of his patient ready. Dr. Whitehall appeared a little bored as he sat in the residents' room listening to Ferg's presentation. Students often wore the same clothes the day after call, since they would not have been home to change, but it appeared that Dr. Whitehall was also dressed the same as the day before. He wore khaki pants, a light blue shirt, a navy-colored tie with ducks on it, and the standard attending's long white lab coat. Although preppie and not unfashionable, it was strikingly like his previous day's attire.

"… and his grandmother died at age eighty-four, probably from a stroke … And, his cousin … "

"That's okay!" interrupted Dr. Whitehall. "Just give me the 'positive' family history and 'pertinent negatives.' I want you to have asked all the questions in your histories, but only relate the pertinent information to me. If I need more details, I will ask you."

"Oh … Yes, sir … er … Negative for cancer, TB, and lung disease … and … positive for asthma in his cousin."

Walter Ferguson continued his presentation on the chronic-bronchitis case, after which he fielded questions from Dr. Whitehall.

"What pathogens are responsible for bacterial bronchitis?"

"Usually it's a mixture of respiratory pathogens found in sputum cultures: Diplococcus pneumonia, Hemophilus influenza, and Mycoplasma pneumonia. Often there is not a predominant organism." Ferg had done his homework.

"That's good. Did you measure the pulsus paradoxus?"

"Ah, … no, sir."

"Can you explain the 'pulsus paradoxus' to me?"

"No, sir. I don't think so."

"Anyone?"

"Yes, sir," Dr. Paul Felton volunteered after a respectful pause. "It's an indirect measure of expiratory effort. It's measured as the difference in the systolic blood pressures taken during expiration and inspiration."

And so began internal medicine—questioning endlessly until there were no more questions or, more likely, no more answers. The winner, the most brilliant physician, appeared to be the one who answered the last question, even if it were his own.

Obie peered into the microscope in the lab on North-7, feeling fully awake even as midnight approached on his first night of medical call. The medicine rotation instilled him with an intellectual high, helping to fend off the physical fatigue. Pinkish cells with irregularly clustered purple nuclei lit up the field. It was incredible that this bright, colorful scene was slimy brown sputum in a plastic cup just five minutes before.

"You see the Gram-positive diplococci?" questioned Larry Forberg, the intern. "They look like grapes in pairs."

"Yeah, I do," answered Obie.

"Pneumococcal pneumonia, classic. The germ named after

'pneumonia.'"

From previous discussions in attending rounds and some reading, Obie remembered the treatment. "Penicillin-G, six hundred thousand units IV QID," he announced.

"Well, …yeah…," whined Dr. Forberg, "but if we use a cephalosporin, we can cover possible Gram-negative organisms as well. I'm going to start him on cefazolin five hundred milligrams Q twelve hours." That made sense to Obie.

The patient had come in from the Blue ER. His IV was already started, blood cultures drawn, and lab reports back … even his arterial blood gas, ABG. Obie did have to run the EKG and interpret it himself. He had time to do his H&P write-up, briefly review differential diagnoses and complications and still get three hours sleep before rounds.

Dr. Whitehall arrived at seven thirty, dressed in khaki pants, light blue shirt, duck tie, and lab coat. Obie was ready to make his presentation.

"Okay, Obie Hardy," he invited. Obie straightened his papers and cleared his throat. "Wait. Let's do this without reading your workup. Give me your write-up first," reaching out to take Obie's papers.

"All right … well … er …" Obie fumbled to organize his thoughts, handing Dr. Whitehall his H&P. "Mr. Snellun is a sixty-eight-year-old black male who presented to the ER with … ah … a two-day history of cough, chills, and brown sputum." He continued his awkward presentation and was struggling to describe the murmur he heard during his cardiac exam.

"Are you describing a systolic ejection-type murmur?" interrupted Dr. Whitehall.

"Ah … yes?" uncertainly.

"Well, you can summarize such findings to make your presentation more concise. If I want more detail, I'll ask for it. Go ahead."

At last, they came to the questions.

"What treatment did you start?"

"We started IV cefazolin," offered Obie.

"But, I thought your Gram stain confirmed Pneumococcal pneumonia. Didn't it?"

"Yes, sir ... but cefazolin has Gram-negative activity ... "

"Yes, yes, I know. But Pneumococcus is exquisitely sensitive to penicillin, which costs less than ten dollars a day. Cefazolin is sixty to eighty dollars a day and, sure, you get extended coverage, but this costs an additional six hundred dollars or more for a course of therapy for drugs alone."

Obie glanced briefly at Dr. Forberg, suppressing his urge to say, "I told you so." The medical team had to function as a team, sharing call, patient care, and admissions, and even responsibility. The team concept even extended to physicians in general and was evidenced by doctors using the term "we" when expressing their opinions. "'We' think you should be hospitalized," or "'We' think you need surgery." The need for a united stand was more critical than the desires of the individuals, especially medical students, who were often less useful than an experienced orderly.

"We'll switch his antibiotic this morning," announced Dr. Forberg to Dr. Whitehall.

Obie completed his scut work, retrieving culture and X-ray results, writing his patient notes, and working up a new admission with pancreatitis and gout. The mental fog of sleep deprivation did not dampen the experience of learning to place a nasogastric tube or draw joint fluid from a knee joint. He did well to finish by six thirty that evening and ride his bike home before dark. Being more fatigued than hungry, he mechanically ate a sub sandwich and drank a Pepsi while he telephoned Priscilla.

"Well, I don't think I'd see much more of you if we were living together," she said.

"I guess you're right, Priss."

"Well, you rest up tonight, because I expect manicotti tomorrow and some decent company."

"Okay. It's a deal. I'm going to take a shower and crash now."

"Okay. I love you."

"Love you too. Goodnight."

The hot shower felt good, but not as good as the bed. Obie glanced over his new patient write-up for morning rounds and set his alarm for six fifteen. He was asleep in minutes. Semi-consciousness returned when his bed shifted slightly. Something warm and soft pressed against him, and he could hear a familiar voice, "If we lived together we could at least sleep together at night."

"Uh-huh," mumbled Obie before consciousness left him again.

In the early morning light, he realized he had not been dreaming. Priscilla had spent the night with him ... sleeping. Fatigue had prohibited any non-somnolent activities, and now impending morning rounds took priority.

"I must have been dead last night," offered Obie.

"I know. I didn't expect anything. I just wanted to be with you. But, tonight may be a different story!"

As they followed Dr. Whitehall and the residents down the hall on rounds, Obie questioned Walter Ferguson. "Do they call internists 'fleas' because they pick at you for information, like fleas biting?"

"I don't know," answered Ferguson. "I thought it was because of all the needle sticks for tests and IVs are like 'fleas' biting and sucking blood."

"*Code blue, North 813 ... Code blue, North 813,*" the hospital intercom announced loudly.

Obie and Walter ran behind Dr. Felton as he bolted up the stairs to the eighth floor. They crowded into the room to watch or help, but the distressed patient was already mobbed by assorted medical residents, interns, nurses, nursing students, and medical students. Obie counted fourteen people attending to the patient in N-813. John Morgan weaved through the crowd, drawn like a magnet to fellow med students.

"Why aren't you in there saving that patient?" asked Walter, "Like a true 'flea'?"

"Well, that patient has breast cancer with bone metastases. I wouldn't have thought they would do CPR on her." Dr. Felton was now over the patient's bed, doing the chest compressions.

"One-and-two-and-three-and-four-and-five," he counted, so the one squeezing the ambu bag could time the inhalations. There were two sounds like popcorn popping during his compressions as ribs broke from the pressure upon her chest. "Is she on narcotics?" he asked. Several people murmured affirmative. "Okay, how about some Narcan?" A nurse responded with a syringe of Narcan, injecting it into the IV. Some ripples appeared on the heart monitor, and the team proceeded with electrical shocks. The medical students squeezed out of the crowded room into the hall. The code continued for several minutes more.

"You know," John said, "I heard they're called 'fleas' because they won't leave a dying dog until long after it's dead."

The picture of the debilitated, dying woman was still haunting Obie as he waited to order his supper. The patient's room had been packed with students of medicine and nursing whose attentions were sharply focused on the death drama that ensued. No medical lecture could have been as stimulating: the beeping sounds of the heart monitor, popping of ribs, and jolting electrical shocks; the sight of the green-lit monitor screen and colored medicine vial boxes; the smell of sputum and burnt flesh. Was this an appropriate learning experience?

At dinner, Obie found himself replaying the scene.

"So, you're mighty quiet tonight. How was your day on the wards?" asked Priscilla. "Probably a zoo, huh?"

"Well, more like a flea circus," responded Obie, returning to the present. "So, what'll it be? The manicotti?"

"I think so. How about some wine?"

"Sure! Let's get a bottle."

Obie felt warm—his stomach full and his head a little light

from the wine.

"My place tonight?" asked Priscilla as they left Bella Italia.

"Sure." Obie realized he would spend the next night on call and then crash on Saturday. He was glad Priscilla was so supportive and was prepared to follow her anywhere tonight. Since he had consumed more wine than she did, Priscilla drove the two miles to her apartment. Obie studied her legs in the car, picturing her upper thighs after they disappeared under her black skirt. He caressed her curved buttocks as they walked into the entrance hallway to her apartment, and, when she had unlocked the door, he pulled her against him and kissed her. The warmth of her body against his and the passion in her kiss made his head reel. They stumbled into the bedroom and continued embracing on her bed. Obie's hand now explored those upper thighs, beneath her skirt, and found the soft, smooth nylon of her panties. She unbuttoned his shirt as he removed her skirt. He popped open the front latch of her bra and released her breasts, round and smooth, nipples erect. The pale beige coloration of the nipple areolae signaled to Obie that Priscilla was nulliparous, never subjected to the pregnancy hormonal bombardment that darkened the nipple pigmentation. As they squirmed under the sheets, their breathing quickened. Obie felt his penis taut against his undershorts, straining with desire. She tugged at his shorts and he pulled them down while placing his face between her breasts. Here, he smelled her sweet perfume and captured one of her nipples in his mouth. He slid off her panties, her pelvis rising up to assist him. He pinned down her body with his.

Brrring!

"The phone!" she cried, squirming out from under him. Trying to control her breathing, she reached over to the bedside table.

Brrring!

"Hello?" She took a breath. "Sure." Another breath. "…He is here." Another breath. "…Would you like to speak to him?" She handed him the phone. "It's your mother!" she whispered and fell back into the bed.

"Mom … Yeah, we went out to dinner." Obie listened to her update on his brother and sisters. She was planning Thanksgiving dinner and wanted him to attend. "Well, Mom, I'll be on my second medicine rotation then. I won't know my schedule until three weeks from now." More questions about Priscilla, if she would be coming, what were their intentions, she wanted grandchildren soon, et cetera … "Well, Mom, it's good to hear from you. I'm on call tomorrow night, so I'll need to be getting some rest tonight … Yeah, I love you too … Good night!"

He turned back to Priscilla, who had put on her panties and his shirt. She was lying on her side, back toward him, chest rising slowly with each breath.

"Priscilla?... Prissy?" he called, softly. She appeared asleep but did attempt to answer.

"Hmmm?" she purred. Obie cuddled up against her back; his erection had waned considerably, but he still longed for fulfillment. He was able to fall asleep, but only after another thirty minutes.

John Morgan was sitting at a table in the cafeteria with a classmate, Kathy Newman. She was short but well proportioned, with shag-cut, brunette hair. He spoke sympathetically to her. "So, it appears that medicine wasn't the best rotation for you to start third year with."

Kathy stared into her coffee, hoping to see something other than reality. "I guess not. A 'marginal' doesn't cut it."

"It doesn't seem fair. All those hours … patient workups."

"Well, my patient workups needed workups."

"How's Bob dealing with this?"

Tears filled her eyes as she looked up at John. "We may be getting separated. He hasn't been home but two days this past week." John thought she appeared pale, like someone suffering a tremendous blood loss. Her emotional life's blood was drained.

"Oh, shit! As if you don't have enough on you! Are you talking to anyone?"

"They 'advised' me to see the school counselor. I've been twice so far."

Obie approached their table with his breakfast tray. "Hi, John. Kathy. So you've got Saturday call duty, too," he said as he sat up to the table.

"Obie," chirped John. "Sure!" He was relieved that the intensity was interrupted.

"Yep. Why not?" added Kathy flatly.

"The 'Skull and Bones' is closed on weekends. What rotation are you on, Kathy?" continued Obie.

"I'm on psych," she replied. Obie noticed a haggard look about her. Psych had not been difficult compared to medicine. Her appearance didn't seem appropriate. "I'll see you guys later," she said, getting up. "I've got to write up a patient. Thanks, John!" She smiled, but only superficially.

"Sure," he replied as Kathy walked off with her tray.

"I thought the psych rotation wasn't so intense," said Obie, when Kathy had left.

"Well, she's having other problems. She's going to have to repeat medicine, and her husband's bagging out."

"Oh, man! I thought that being a physical therapist would make medical school easier for her. I had no idea."

"Well, maybe she'll work things out." John patted Obie's shoulder as he stood, taking his coffee cup in his other hand. "I'll check you later."

"Okay, man. See you." Obie seemed to be more emotional after a night on call. Somehow, the sleep deprivation emotionally weakened him, making him more vulnerable to his feelings. He was sad for Kathy and sensed his eyes filling with water. He had not seen Priscilla since the night of their coitus interruptus, and suddenly he longed for her ... not sexually, just to touch her, hug her, and feel the warmth and security she brought to him. *I'll call Prissy as soon as I'm done,* he thought. *Maybe she'll let me crash at her place tonight.*

Attending rounds were brief Saturday—only emergency X-ray studies and the most routine lab tests were performed on weekends, and therefore less scut work for the studs. Dr. Whitehall was certainly not anxious to spend much of his weekend at the hospital, and he restricted his discussions to basic medical-care concerns. Obie was ready to leave before one p.m. He called Priscilla from the residents' room.

"Hey, baby. I'm done!"

"Well, this is early," she replied with a yawn. "I've just been up a couple of hours."

"How about me coming over to your place to sleep a while? Would I be in your way?"

"No, I'll just do some laundry or something."

"Great! Let's see, if I bike home and get my car … "

"Don't bother. I'll pick you up in fifteen minutes."

"Great! Thanks, Priss."

Twenty minutes later, her blue Sunbird stopped on Twelfth Street beside the three bears statue. Obie squinted at the bright daylight flooding his tired eyes. He hopped in the car, carrying his blue, nylon knapsack.

"Hmmph! You stink!" greeted Priscilla, wrinkling her nose.

"Sorry. I hadn't noticed. I guess thirty-six hours in the same clothes does build up. Thanks for picking me up."

"Sure. Have you had lunch?"

"No, not yet. Are you hungry?"

"Well, I could eat a doughnut." She smiled at Obie.

The traffic was light on Saturday, and they arrived at the Dunkin' Donuts on Midlothian Turnpike in no time. Over the soup and donut special, Obie told Priscilla about Kathy Newman. Priscilla worked in the medical-school media center and knew most of his classmates.

"She's seeing a school counselor," he said.

"I hope she doesn't drop out," said Priscilla. She knew that the class had been thinned from its initial 180 members. "How many are in your class now?"

"About 172," answered Obie. "Thirty percent female."

"In a lot of ways, it's more difficult for a woman to pursue a professional career like medicine."

"I reckon so. Many men are too macho to grocery shop, cook, or do laundry. I'm sure Kathy has had to do all that stuff too. Am I that macho?"

"No," laughed Priscilla. "You're 'muncho'!" She smiled and bit at his chest.

Monday was busy on the wards. Diagnostic tests on the weekend admissions had to be performed, the daily patient care attended to, and the new medical problems had to be studied by the students. In addition, Obie had a new patient workup to prepare. It was a long day, and Obie didn't get a break until 9:30 p.m., only to read up on asthma management for Tuesday rounds.

Dr. Whitehall arrived Tuesday morning dressed in khaki pants, light blue shirt, and a navy tie with ducks. Obie had studied his asthma medications, the biochemical actions and side effects. His patient workup was recorded in note form on his three-by-five index card. He wanted to impress the attending, who had listened to his presentation attentively. Obie even included the pulsus paradoxus. Dr. Whitehall nodded and asked about the complications of corticosteroids, which the patient was receiving. Obie listed the side effects, including glucose intolerance, fluid retention, behavioral changes, increased appetite, decreased resistance to infection, and stomach ulcers.

"Do steroids cause ulcers?" asked Dr. Whitehall.

"Ah … yes, they can," offered Obie.

"It's interesting that you say that. Indeed, patients on steroids develop ulcerations in the stomach, but the steroids are only a factor, not a cause. The resistance of the gastric mucosa to ulceration is lowered by the steroid administration. This does not cause the ulcers itself without acid, stress, sympathetic tone, and other medications." The group nodded, understandingly. "Now, since they can suppress the adrenals and affect other glands, can you describe this patient's endocrine exam?"

Obie was blindsided—the endocrine exam? He should have expected this from an endocrinologist. He tried to organize his thoughts but only fumbled the response, "Endocrine exam?"

"Yes, the endocrine exam." Obie could only think of the pancreas, the adrenals, and the pituitary glands—none of which were accessible to physical examination. *The thyroid! That's an endocrine gland!*

"Er … the neck showed no thyromegally," Obie timidly offered. Dr. Whitehall nodded approvingly. *The gonads! They were some more glands!* "And, the testicles were firm; descended bilaterally, without masses."

"Good," said Dr. Whitehall. "Now, there are other systemic findings related to endocrine pathology. There's hirsutism, trunkal obesity, gynecomastia, and skin thickness or striae."

Obie had recovered some of his sleep by Wednesday, which was Halloween. The M-81s were having a Halloween party on Grace Street near the VCU campus in Larry Hall's apartment. Obie and Priscilla had bought two rubber masks at Hecks over the weekend and donned these with sheets gathered over their heads like hoods. He hadn't wanted to party during the week, especially while on medicine rotation, but when they arrived, he was glad they came. Larry was in rare form, wearing a giant yellow cardboard circle with "Roche @" printed on it. Priscilla and Obie looked at him, appearing puzzled.

"Valium," Larry said smiling. "Diazepam." He then turned his back to them, displaying a large numeral five. "Five milligrams!" He laughed and then disappeared into the crowd. Cheryl Wright was breathtaking in her prostitute outfit—a red miniskirt slit along the side with black, fishnet stockings. There were several toga costumes, a Roman gladiator with sword, and a balding male student clad only in a giant diaper, carrying a giant bottle and puffing on a cigar. Everyone was happy, dancing, and drinking beer. It was a delightful contrast to the rigid, cerebral air that the student doctors took on in the hospital. John walked up to them, wearing overalls, a straw hat, and chewing on a blade of straw.

"Obie! Good to see you! And Priscilla."

"Hey, John. Did Samantha come with you?"

"Yeah. Sam's around here somewhere. There she is!" He pointed to a tall woman in bib overalls with freckles painted on her cheeks, smoking a cigar. "Sam!" She moved across the room toward them.

"Is that a cigar?" asked Priscilla.

"Yeah. That's how we met. We were both in ROTC and at summer camp playing army. Some of the guys stepped out to smoke cigars, and she joined us." Sam was grinning as she heard his story and stood beside him. They appeared an odd couple. She was all of five foot nine, puffing a cigar, standing above John's five foot seven. Kathy Newman stumbled along beside them, her toga disheveled, but she was smiling brightly, sloshing beer from her plastic cup.

"Hi, guys!" she greeted with a giggle and hung momentarily onto John's shoulder; she then staggered off into the partiers.

"Well, she looks in better spirits!" said Obie.

"Yeah," John said, but his eyes had lost their usual sparkle. He was worried, thinking that maybe she'd given up hope all together.

When they left the party, Obie drove Priscilla to her apartment, assuming they would bed down at the closest of their residences. He had his sheet wrapped tightly around his shoulders to fend off the autumn night chill.

"How'd you like the party?" he asked.

"Well, it's the most fun I've had under these sheets in a while!"

"Oh, yeah? Well, maybe I can improve on that!"

"Well, you'll probably want to wait another four or five days. Even though it's Halloween, I'm not too fond of bloodstains on my sheets."

Obie considered just going back to his place for the night, thinking how frustrating it would be to try to sleep with her without sexual fulfillment. Tomorrow night he'd be on call; the next night would be recovery. He wouldn't see much of her for the next three days, and he would have another seven miles to drive back to the Coop.

"You're welcome to stay with me, anyway," she offered. It was enough to sway his decision.

"Okay," he replied as he thought to himself, *Great, another asexual night! And they call us "studs."*

On morning rounds, the studs straggled a little behind the medical team. Ferg whispered to Obie, "Hey, the Halloween party gave me an idea. What if we all dressed like Dr. Whitehall on Monday?"

"Yeah. I've got a navy duck tie. I'm game. Do you think he'll notice?"

"Who cares? Are you going into endocrinology?"

"I don't think so!"

They were able to convince the JAR, Dr. Felton, to join in the masquerade. Monday morning found three members of the medical team clad in light blue shirts, khakis, and navy blue ties. Dr. Whitehall was true to form, arriving in his well-established prep-suit. He did comment on how preppie Dr. Felton looked and, on rounds, stated how much like a "team" they had become. Obie and Ferg could hardly refrain from bursting out with laughter. Apparently, their prank was not unnoticed, because the next day, Dr. Whitehall wore a burgundy tie. This, however, was difficult for him, since he adjusted and fidgeted with it all morning, and, the following day, he returned, wearing the navy tie … with ducks.

Ward 4, Cardiology, at the Veterans Hospital

Chapter 6
Ward 4–Cardiology

One third of the first clinical year for the M-81s was over. The second medicine rotation found Obie returning to the McGuire Veterans Administration Hospital, the "VA", Ward 4, cardiology. The ward was in the far northwest corner of the hospital complex, some distance from the hub and even further from A&D. Again, Cheryl Wright was teamed with Obie, as well as Jim Beam. Jim was a handsome young man with straight, light brown hair with a few streaks of sun-bleached blond. Had his wire-rimmed glasses been sunshades, one could picture him on the beach with a surfboard. He had been dating Cheryl for a year or so.

"Well, how did you two manage to get the same assignments?" asked Obie.

"We had to pull a few strings with the clinical coordinators," replied Jim.

"Yeah, unfortunately," added Cheryl.

"Unfortunately?" Obie wondered aloud.

"Yeah," she continued. "We thought this way we could see more of each other. However, we have to take call on different nights. That gives us only one or two nights a week when we're off at the same time."

"I see. Bummer." Obie knew how academically competitive med students were, and that they tended to be compared to other students on the same rotation. This could create friction in a relationship as each tried to outshine the other in the eyes of their attending physician. Most of Jim and Cheryl's time together would now be in an environment where one's performance reflected inversely upon the other.

There were two interns and a JAR on the cardiology service. Sara Leming was the JAR. She was smallish, early thirties, with sharp but nicely shaped features. Her hair was sandy and cut in a short shag. Her interns were Crystal Meriwether and David Morningstar. A cardiology fellow had his own office adjacent to the Cardiac Intensive Care Unit, the CICU. He was black, but not Afro-American. His features and accent were Caribbean in flavor. Clarence Strong was head of the team, even though he reported to the attending. The team met in a room off the back of the CICU. There were several electronic machines shoved into one corner with switches, wires running about, and black video monitors. The students were introduced to everyone as new recruits to the cardiology team.

Sara Leming led the team on walking rounds. Dr. Strong accompanied the team only in the CICU, and then excused himself to his office. There was a large room with six patients across the hall from the nurses' station. Three large windows along the outside wall illuminated the room beyond that of the ceiling lights.

"And this is our 'garden room,'" announced Dr. Leming.

"Is it because it's so bright?" asked Cheryl.

"Nope."

"Because the patients are being fed and watered?" offered Obie.

"Nope. Because it's full of 'vegetables'!" she explained as she turned and led them into the room. Three patients were, indeed, asleep. One mechanically followed their movements with empty eyes while another stared at the ceiling. The sixth patient was lying on his side, facing the windows. Dr. Leming gestured at him. "Note the phototropism."

Herman Scott weighed over 350 pounds, the limit of the medical scales. His eyes slowly closed, and his head drooped forward as Obie attempted to extract his medical history.

"Snorkkh ..." (exhale) . . . snorkkh . . ."

"Mr. Scott!" Obie called, "Herman Scott! Are you allergic to any medicines?"

"Huh?" His eyes opened. "Ah ... no, no allergies ..." His eyes drifted down. "Snorkkh ..." (exhale) ... snorkkh ..."

"Mr. Scott! Herman! Have you ever had any surgery?"

"Huh? ... Ah, ... Tonsils, two years ago." His face was engorged and purplish; his lower lip was so swollen with edema that clear fluid oozed through the skin surface in places. Sleep engulfed him again. Obie was unfamiliar with Pickwickian Syndrome, also known as sleep apnea, where a combination of obesity, lung disease, and upper airway obstruction lead to short periods of sleep that abruptly end with arrests in the breathing.

"The excessive abdominal tissue restricts movement of the diaphragm. Oxygen levels run low, carbon dioxide high," explained Dr. Leming. "Treatment involves significant weight reduction and removing the upper airway obstruction by tonsillectomy and, as a last resort, tracheostomy. I've ordered a twelve-hundred-calorie diet."

The next day on rounds, Dr. Leming asked about Mr. Scott's respiratory rate and weight.

"Well, he weighs above the limits of the ward scales," explained Obie.

"I've checked with administration. We can have him taken to the laundry room and weighed each day. The laundry scales go up to a thousand pounds," offered Dr. Leming. "Mr. Scott, how are you doing on the diet? Are you comfortable?"

"Sure, no problem," he answered.

As they walked off, Dr. Leming addressed the intern, Dr. Morningstar, "Decrease his diet to one thousand calories."

The next patient they addressed had congestive heart failure, and his body fluid needed careful monitoring. Dr, Leming asked Dr. Morningstar, "What's his weight today?"

"Er … I don't know. I can get his chart and look."

"You should know your patient's weight if you're treating him for congestive failure."

"Well, I can bring the charts with me on rounds," offered Dr. Morningstar.

"Whatever it takes." Dr. Leming moved on to the next patient, but her disgust was quite apparent.

The following morning, Obie was able to report that Mr. Scott's weight was 384 pounds, more than the weight of the entire Ward 4 linens, including towels.

"Mr. Scott. How are you doing with this diet?" queried Dr. Leming. "Are you staying hungry?"

"It's okay."

Dr. Leming nodded but said to Morningstar as they left the bedside, "Decrease his diet to eight hundred calories." Again, at the next bed, she asked, "His weight today?"

Dr. Morningstar shuffled through the dozen of charts he was carrying. Three charts cascaded to the floor, and Obie reached down to pick these up.

"Er … I'll find it in a minute," he replied.

"Here it is," said Obie, holding out the opened chart for Dr. Morningstar. "192 pounds."

"Yeah. 192 pounds," continued Morningstar.

"What's his dig level?" she asked.

"Ah … " he fumbled through the chart Obie was holding. "Yeah, it's 1.2."

She stared grimly at Dr. Morningstar for an eternal few

seconds before turning silently and proceeding to the next patient. She stepped beside the next patient's bed and addressed Obie, ignoring the presence of the intern.

"What did Mr. Kline's thallium scan show?"

"I don't know. He's not my patient," replied Obie, looking at Dr. Morningstar to signal his cue.

"Ah …" Dr. Morningstar paused, flipping through the pages of the medical record. "… The report's not back yet."

Dr. Leming's voice, devoid of emotion, retorted, "His scan was done yesterday. We need the results to make his disposition. Obie, can you get it immediately after rounds?"

"Sure!" He was delighted that his assistance was requested Bestowing this responsibility upon him made him feel accepted as a member of the medical team, a valuable contributor to the management of their patients. He felt a little uncomfortable being positioned in the middle of the Leming-Morningstar antagonism. He looked up at Dr. Morningstar, seeking a reassuring or accepting expression. Dr. Morningstar appeared unaffected by the request, as if business as usual prevailed.

After rounds, Dr. Morningstar took his patient charts and headed for the nursing station to write the new orders as Dr. Leming touched Obie's arm, signaling him to lag behind.

"As of now," she announced, "*All* the patients are 'yours.' I want you to follow *all* of them for me."

"Okay," replied Obie slowly, uncertain of this added responsibility, but certain that he could not refuse the request of the JAR.

"Don't worry. Just get three-by-five cards on everyone and track their medications, vital signs, and test results. Being an intern isn't as complicated as all that," she said, gesturing in the direction that Dr. Morningstar disappeared in. "I'll sign any orders you want to write on them."

Attending rounds were held in the back room off from the CICU. Dr. Strong, the fellow, functioned as the attending. He gave medical household hints, or "pearls," as guidance on patient management and medical philosophy of varying usefulness. He was, essentially, student teaching for the attending, Dr. Cavale. Dr. Cavale was an eastern Indian man, about forty with a neatly trimmed mustache. Cheryl Wright was completing her presentation of a patient with chest pain. Usually the attending would discuss the management of each new admission, but she offered an addendum.

"Ah … I was reading in *Harrison's Textbook of Medicine* about stress testing. Apparently, with atypical chest pain, there is a high incidence of false negative stress tests, as high as 20 percent. With thallium-201 nuclear scanning added to the test, the sensitivity and specificity for significant coronary stenosis is over 90 percent. Since this patient's symptoms are atypical for classical angina, I feel that he should have a stress-thallium exercise test."

"Thank you. That is most accurate," commented Dr. Strong. Cheryl feigned modesty as her ego absorbed the praise like a sponge, swelling to a fullness inside her. Jim Beam smiled weakly, happy for his girlfriend's presentation but wondering how he would compare. After rounds, he quickly excused himself to go start a new patient workup.

Jim Beam was prepared for his patient presentation the following morning on congestive heart failure. After his H&P recitation, he reported, "I reviewed a recent article in August's *Annals of Internal Medicine* reporting the use of angiotensin converting enzymes for congestive heart failure. They used Captopril in low doses while monitoring renal function closely. It appears to be a significant benefit to its use over digoxin and diuretics alone."

"Yes …" began Dr. Strong, editorializing this summary. "Captopril has great promise in treating hypertension and, possibly, as the article alludes, in CHF. Unfortunately, however, we have no investigational drug studies to supply us and we'll have to wait six to twelve months for FDA approval. But thank you for that abstract review. It is most timely." Dr. Cavale nodded approvingly before he adjourned himself to the cardiac cath lab. Jim felt satisfied with his performance, but, since no patient-management recommendations resulted from his work, he felt his achievement was somewhat empty.

Sunday rounds were abbreviated, all business and little cerebralizing, so that the medical team members not on call could escape early. Dr. Leming recommended sit-down rounds in the cafeteria over coffee and Danishes for the on-call team. They sat at a table by the glass wall over-looking the arcade. Dr. Leming, Dr. Morningstar, and Obie perused their three-by-five patient cards like poker players vying for the pot.

"So ... Mr. Laser needs a gated pool scan Monday and possible discharge Tuesday," opened Dr. Leming.

"Okay," responded Dr. Morningstar.

"And Mr. Gentry's still on the transplant list," continued Obie.

"What? Is that? I don't believe it!" exclaimed Sara Leming, her eyes suddenly wider than any coffee could make them. "Look over there!" she continued, almost whispering now.

"Herman Scott," stated Morningstar, identifying his morbidly obese, Pickwickian patient. Mr. Scott sat at a table, also overlooking the arcade, with a large cup of coffee and four glazed doughnuts stacked on his plate. He was contently chewing on a fifth doughnut.

"No wonder he hasn't complained about the eight-hundred-calorie diet!" exclaimed Leming.

Beep-beep-beep!

"Well, it looks like our first admission's in A&D."

"I was going to check the orders on the ward," said Morningstar. "Maybe I can restrict Mr. Scott's cafeteria privileges."

"Okay," responded Leming, happy to be unburdened of the intern. "I'll be in A&D ... Hardy, why don't you come with me?"

"Okay."

Obie carefully surveyed A&D, noting how tiny it was

compared to the MCV Blue ER. There was only room for six stretchers, with the nursing and doctors station at the far end. He studied the glass walls and chilled slightly as he remembered Cheryl's encounter with the pistol-toting, psychotic husband. This was certainly close quarters for a shoot-out.

Dr. Leming was directed to a stretcher along the back wall, a Mr. Paschall. Obie accompanied her to the bedside and observed her H&P. He would have to repeat this in much greater detail later. The cardiac monitor overhead displayed a continuous stream of green, luminous, electrical heartbeat tracings. Obie noted an occasional wide, large irregularity in the pattern that he identified as PVCs, or premature ventricular contractions. This signified some type of irritability in the heart. As Dr. Leming did the heart exam, he wondered about the tan-colored rubber sheath on the bell of her stethoscope. He gestured inquisitively at it as they returned to the doctors station.

"Oh, that? It's a baby's nipple," she explained, holding it out for Obie to examine. "Some of these emphysematous old men have such bony rib cages that I need a rubber rim to get good chest-wall contact."

"Oh. Neat."

"Well, this looks like a CCU admission, Hardy. Rule out MI. We'll need to take him to X-ray first. Let me write a quick note."

Obie began his physical in the meantime, listening to Mr. Paschall's heart and lungs, palpating his abdomen, and checking his legs for swelling and pulses. He pulled out his reflex hammer when he was interrupted by a hand on his shoulder.

"Ready to move out?" asked Leming.

"Sure."

"Mr. Paschall, we'll be taking you by X-ray and then to your bed in the cardiac intensive care unit," explained Leming.

"Okay," he responded, a little groggy from his morphine injection.

"Hardy, I'll go with you to the arcade. Then I'll need to go clear a bed for him. You'll need to roll him to X-ray, then bring him down to CCU."

Obie was a bit frightened at the thought of being alone in the hall with an intensive care patient, travelling the long corridors of the VAH. He looked at Dr. Leming with uncertainty, "To X-ray?"

Dr. Leming placed the monitor on the stretcher and had a red metal box placed on the shelf below. "Sure," she answered assuredly, as they rolled the stretcher out into the hall. "You'll be fine. You've got this code box if anything happens."

"Well … "

"You know what to do," she continued. "Say his pulse rate drops and his blood pressure falls. What do you do?"

"Ah … ," Obie thought but answered reflexively, "give Atropine?"

"Sure! How about more frequent PVCs?"

"Well, … give IV lidocaine … "

"Yes! How much?" she drilled.

"Uh, … fifty to one hundred milligrams; about one milligram per kilogram."

"Great! All right, V. fib?"

"Shock?"

"Sure. Two hundred joules. The paddles are on the monitor here. See?"

"Uh-huh."

"The ambu bag, epinephrine, bicarb, et cetera, are all here." They were turning the corner onto the arcade now. "Any problems, just page me. You'll do fine." She smiled and moved off to the left, disappearing through the doorway at the corridor entrance.

Obie struggled to keep the stretcher rolling straight as he headed down the long hallway. Yellow ceramic tiles lined the lower half of the walls. *Follow the yellow brick road,* he thought, and then found himself whispering, "We're not in Kansas anymore, Toto."

"What?" asked Mr. Paschall.

"Oh, nothing," he answered. "How are you doing? Any pain?" he asked, trying to sound like he was in charge.

"No problems."

"Good," responded Obie as he navigated a right turn to head for the radiology department. He kept glancing at the monitor screen, hoping the electrical patterns did not change. He watched Mr. Paschall's chest rise with each inspiration, assuring himself that the breathing was continuing. At X-ray, he took another blood-pressure reading, remembering Dr. Leming's scenario of falling blood pressure—134/82. Good! The technician took forever to shoot the film and develop it. Obie hypnotically watched the monitor. When the film was finally ready, he didn't even pause to look at it. He did, however, take another blood-pressure reading before starting down the yellow brick road. It was probably three hundred yards from Radiology to Ward 4, and he would then need to ride the elevator up to the second floor.

A yellow, electric, motorized cart met and passed them in the corridor. These more efficient transport vehicles usually carried a member of the indispensable janitorial department. He heard the bell ring behind him, signaling as the cart turned the corner toward the arcade. Its humming faded out. The hall was quiet again. As he continued to watch the heart monitor, Obie suddenly realized that maybe there were other complications Dr. Leming didn't review. What about atrial fibrillation? Or supraventricular tachycardia? Or complete heart block? *Okay, think.* Atrial fibrillation, what would it do to him? Low blood pressure? Would atropine help this too? No … no. Maybe something to slow down the rate, like digoxin or propranolol. But which one? And, asystole … how would he call a "code blue" out in the hallway? He was relieved to see the elevator just up ahead and noticed the rapidity of his pace. Had he been jogging up the hall?

"Almost there, Mr. Paschall," he said, trying to sound reassuring to both the patient and himself.

When the elevator doors opened onto Ward 4, Obie was certain they were safe. He could get that stretcher the twenty-five or thirty yards to the CCU in seconds if his patient's heart arrested now. Dr. Leming met him as he entered the CCU doors.

"Hardy, that was quick. Any problems?"

"Nope." He smiled, hoping the fine tremor in his legs was not visible to the JAR. "I'll be back in a few minutes," he continued as they rolled Mr. Paschall into bed number four. He wanted to ask her about atrial fibrillation, but the morning coffee had stimulated his colon, and he felt an urgent need to evacuate. An unburdening sigh escaped as he unjacketed in the call-room toilet. His legs felt weak, but were no longer quivering. As he sat on the toilet seat, a wave of relaxation spread over his body from his legs and arms to his rectum, initiating the process of defecation.

"*Code blue, CCU 4 ... Code blue, CCU 4*," the intercom blared out as doors slammed, feet scuffled, and cart wheels squeaked on the tile floor just outside the bathroom.

Chapter 7
Holidays

The drone of conversation, laughter, and children playing underfoot hypnotically relaxed Obie as he sat on his mother's couch, holding a cold beer. Having been on call the previous night, rounded this morning, and traveled the hundred miles from Richmond, his energy supply was depleted. He absorbed the holiday warmth of his family like a motionless iguana basking on a sunny rock. It was difficult to jump into the Thanksgiving social activity, but he was more thankful to be present than he could remember. His growing nieces and nephews were bright, happy, and cheerful. The fireplace flames sparkled in their eyes, so full of life. And Obie, too weak to move from his seat, grew more sedate with each sip of beer. He hoped they didn't think he was unsociable; it just felt so good not to have to think—not to have to worry about another admission or about lab results that weren't on the chart—to hear conversation that didn't involve diseases, complications, and morbidity and mortality. He felt a squeeze on his thigh.

"Hey, are you still with us?" cooed Priscilla.

"Uh-huh, sure," he responded. He noticed his lips were a little numb and hoped his speech was not slurred. The 6 percent ethanol in his beer had sedated Obie, already weakened by fatigue, as much as any narcotic. He hoped his taste buds were not too anesthetized to enjoy the flavors that should follow the delightful aromas he smelled. The turkey dressing, asparagus casserole, home baked rolls, sweet potatoes, and corn pudding had already created an olfactory feast. "I'm still here."

"You could've fooled me," she said, noting his glassy stare and placid smile "I'm starved! Everything smells so good!"

"Yep. I'm enjoying it already." Obie studied her lightly freckled face, so warm and wholesome. Her eyes were dark brown and rich as a loving puppy's. He smiled lovingly at her and hugged her, saying, "Animal eyes."

Priscilla was amused, recognizing the hypnotic state he had entered. "You want another beer?" she inquired. "I'm driving us back home tonight."

"Sure." He smiled, thinking that he was really home already. People *lived* here. People just seemed to be *staying* in the city.

"Obie," said Charlene, his youngest sister, standing in front of him and wiggling the fingers on her outstretched left hand. "Mark and I are getting married in July."

"That's great, Charley! Congratulations!" he answered, standing to hug her and focusing his gaze on the glittering diamond.

"Yeah," added Mark matter-of-factly. "I wanted to wait 'til Christmas to give her the ring, but she'd still have wanted a Christmas present too. This way the engagement won't be lost in all the Christmas activities."

"I know what you mean," responded Obie, reaching to shake Mark's hand. "I hope you know what you're in for!"

"I guess I'll find out."

"Okay everyone, let's eat!" announced Mrs. Hardy.

Kathy Newman sat alone at a formica table in the basement cafeteria of MCV Hospital. She stared at her circular-shaped meat entrée that was masquerading as turkey. Her husband had left the previous day to spend the holiday with his "family". Her hospital work had taken until one o'clock, and she was now preparing a presentation for extra credit. She desperately needed a good grade in psych now. Her plate blurred from the watering in her eyes as she gazed at it, not from the reality of her chair, but from some other place. Her soul was distant, lost in a fog of depression and self-worthlessness. She sniffed and dried her eyes, uncapping a bottle of diazepam sedatives. Her trembling hands jiggled out a pill, and she started to recap the bottle, but dumped out two more pills instead. Standing up to leave, she swallowed the three tablets and smiled as she anticipated some relief from the agony that choked her heart. She walked out into the cold city night to catch the bus to her empty apartment, littered with dirty laundry and junk mail scattered among her medical notes and textbooks.

Friday morning, Larry Hall missed Kathy on psychiatric rounds, especially since he knew she had been intensively preparing her presentation. The team assumed she was ill, maybe even the "monthlies." Larry was even more concerned, having noticed her depressed mood. He tried phoning her apartment after rounds. There was no answer. *Oh well,* he thought, *maybe she went home late for Thanksgiving. That would probably be good for her anyway.*

Bob Newman returned to his apartment shortly before one. It irritated him to find it in such disarray. Two medical textbooks lay opened on the dining room table, with three-by-five index cards scattered about. Something, however, seemed odd to him. He then heard a sound in the bedroom.

"Kathy?" he called, "Are you home?" He walked into the bedroom. His wife was unconscious, lying clothed on top of the bed. "Jee-sus Christ!" he exclaimed. She made loud snoring noises as she breathed and the pungent odor of alcohol filled the room. His eyes blurred from the tears filling them, straining to focus on the empty pill bottle on the floor. He picked up the bottle and put it in his pocket. A frightening feeling squeezed his abdomen and he realized he couldn't sit still and wait for an ambulance, even if he could manage to phone for one. He had to do something now—anything! Struggling with his wife's limp body, he managed to drape her over his shoulder and carry her to his car. MCV was as close to Jarrett Apartments as any other Richmond hospital, and the route was the most familiar. Within minutes, he reached the major medical, Blue ER, entrance off Marshall Street. Kathy was still breathing when they rolled her in on a stretcher. Bob managed to relay the necessary information to the registration clerk while Kathy was having her stomach pumped and toxicology studies performed. He handed the empty bottle to the clerk and went out to move his car. As he sat behind the wheel, he looked at the empty passenger seat where he last saw his wife and began to weep uncontrollably.

Kathy Newman sat, nervously wringing her hands in her lap—hands still stained with yellowish bruises from IVs and phlebotomies. Dean Feldstein's face was stern and glaring as Kathy struggled to maintain eye contact. Sensing her vulnerability, he softened his manner and addressed her sympathetically.

"Kathy, I don't want to belittle the seriousness of your current position. The school invests an enormous amount in each medical student." This was true, since top-notch instructors were not cheap and required state-of-the-art clinical and research facilities to attract. Student tuitions in no way provided the financial support necessary to operate a nationally recognized medical university. The admissions process and selection of student applicants was also costly. "It's to our advantage to see that you graduate with your doctorate degree, even if it means an extra year of training. It's still possible for you to complete third year on schedule and still graduate with your fellow M-81s." She nodded understandingly, feeling a miniscule amount of relief.

"It may be easier on you now to sit out the rest of this year, get yourself together, and start back with the M-82s in July. Your work so far would even give you an edge on the rest of the class."

Just like being a certified physical therapist gave me an edge on my fellow classmates now, she thought to herself. "Thanks, Dr. Feldstein, but my classmates are my friends and peers. If I'm going to make it at all, I'll need their support and my pride. I want to continue now, if I can." She now watched his face, expectantly.

"Okay," he replied softly after a pensive pause. "It won't be easy, …academically or emotionally. Is your husband supportive of this?"

"Yes, he is," she lied, assuming his recent attentiveness was due to support and not apprehension of another crisis. "He's been by my side, faithfully, since Thanksgiving."

Dean Feldstein glanced at the empty chair bedside Kathy but continued, "You must receive counseling, *must*. I will require weekly reports from your therapist, Dr. Swartzman, for the first six weeks—then twice a month. I hate to sound like a probation officer, but I have to know you are well enough to endure the stresses of clinical medicine. You know that physicians have ten times the risk of suicide than the general population."

"Yes, sir."

"And, Kathy, … please come by and talk whenever you like. I *am* on your side, you know. I'll do whatever I can to get you that 'MD'."

"Thank you, sir." She was reassured by his paternal manner. Having feared expulsion, she saw a glimmer of hope in her future. She wished Bob had been present to share this feeling.

"Mr. Newman, come on in. Have a seat," greeted Alan Bedlander, a middle-aged man in a crisp, tailored, charcoal business suit and burgundy silk tie with a gold tie bar and tie clip. "So you're thinking about filing for …"

"Divorce," replied Bob Newman, sitting down across the heavy walnut desk.

"Well, okay. Let's see just how we'll proceed. Do you have grounds for divorce? Infidelity, or such?"

"I'm not sure. It's been difficult since she entered medical school. She studied to two a.m. the first two years and took exams on Saturdays. Now, she stays on the wards overnight every third night. She's always too tired to go out. Too tired to wash clothes. Too tired to vacuum. And, well, I guess, too tired to make love."

"Hmm … not exactly abandonment. Do you suspect she's having an affair, maybe another student on the ward?"

"No, I don't think so. But…" He paused, the tears welling up in his eyes. "… she OD'd Thanksgiving and has become an alcoholic." He felt like he had betrayed his best friend by this disclosure. His stomach knotted, and there was a pressure in his chest.

"Well, I think we have something to work with now!" Alan Bedlander's eyes twinkled as he began to mentally formulate the case. Bob Newman felt dizzy and nauseated. The attorney noticed his client's pale complexion. "Oh, would you like some water or something, Mr. Newman?"

"Yes," replied Bob, weakly. "I think so." He was lightheaded and felt the blood pulsing in his temples. His Episcopal upbringing had instilled him with a divine regard for matrimony—a union in the eyes of God. Mr. Bedlander could legally sever the bond of marriage, but he had pledged his soul to Kathy. Divorce was, to him, a sin; but then, so was suicide. He still cared for Kathy, so much so that each day he dreaded going home, afraid of what he might find. Scooping her up from the edge of death was an exhausting experience. It was a responsibility he could not bear every day.

"Are you sure you really want a divorce?" asked Bedlander, handing him a paper cup.

"I'm not 100 percent sure," he heard himself say. "It will

probably end up that way. I just want to have the paperwork started so that I can proceed quickly. Maybe it won't be as difficult then."

"Okay, I understand." Mr. Bedlander paused to structure his recommendation. "I'll draw up a legal separation with the date left blank on grounds of 'mental instability.' You can come by and review the papers in two weeks. I'd rather not mail them in case your wife was to open them accidentally."

"All right, thank you. That sounds fine." Bob Newman stood, his legs slightly trembling, feeling as though his burden had been lightened. Someone was helping him carry the load. "I'll see you in two weeks," he said, shaking Mr. Bedlander's hand.

Kathy burst through the apartment door, calling cheerfully, "Bob! … Bob! You home?"

"Sure."

"I'm still an M-3! I can still finish by '81!"

"Really? That's great!" he replied, successfully hiding his ambivalence.

"Yeah! …But I gotta go to counseling and still repeat medicine this summer. It won't be easy, but I can do it!" She jumped to him and wrapped her arms around his torso.

"Sure you can, babe," he responded automatically, returning her embrace and trying to absorb and share some of her excitement. Maybe everything will be okay. She slid her arms under his shirt, and he felt her warm hands on his back and then stroke his chest hair. Her eyes had a lusty sparkle as she smiled at him. It had been two months since they last had sex, and then only when she had awakened him at three a.m., needing a stress relief from her all-night studying session. She laughed as she led him to the bedroom. Their caressing increased as their clothing decreased. His chest sported a healthy crop of sandy colored curls, matching his coarse hair and thick mustache. His hand glided over the nylon surface of her pantyhose and then helped cast off her blouse. He suddenly noticed the needle marks on her hands and forearms and remembered her limp body on the same bed hardly a week ago. She felt the growing firmness in his crotch.

"And to think you were talking about separation," she purred.

Despite how much he wanted to show his support and how much he wanted to forget the past few months, he couldn't maintain his erection. His internal unrest had neutralized his libido. He managed to conceal this somewhat by providing masturbatory stimulation to his partner until her body jerked spasmodically into orgasm. She was physically relieved, but her vagina longed to be filled with her husband's warm, pulsating organ. There was an emptiness still, as she lay beside her lover. His arousal had never been lacking before. Bob Newman also felt vacant as he lay with Kathy in his arms.

John Morgan had curiously anticipated Thursday evening since he had received the letter with its rich, raised letterhead. As he sat in George Ben Johnson auditorium, he chatted with several of his classmates. Cheryl Wright, Harvey Barton, and the class president, Ralph Walton, were there. He recognized a few fourth-year medical students present. Dean Feldstein was down in front of the amphitheater-styled auditorium and called for order to begin the ceremony.

"You all have been invited here tonight to acknowledge exceptional performance and leadership displayed in the field of medicine. We have thirty-two new members to be inducted tonight, twenty-eight from the M-81, third-year class. 'AOA' is the honor society recognizing academic excellence in medical education. You new members tonight have been selected for both scholastic standing and demonstration of leadership qualities as noted by your teachers. AOA is Alpha Omega Alpha, the first and last letters of the Greek alphabet. It is symbolic of beginning to end, completeness, and beginning again, …going the extra distance, …teaching another who is beginning—as did the Greek physician, Hippocrates, 'Father of Medicine,' even in the fifth century BC."

John was beaming as his candle was lit, standing down in front of the auditorium, alongside his classmates. He was pleased that someone would notice him, a man from the rural Blue Ridge Mountains, in such a ceremonious manner. Dazzled by the formality and reverence of this ritual, he had not even considered the impact this honor would have on his selection of residencies.

Cheryl's head was still drifting in the clouds when she reached her apartment. Jim Beam had been waiting for her.

"Well, what was it all about?" he queried, excitedly as she entered.

"Oh, well, … it's some sort of honor society," she explained, handing him her certificate. "The 'AOA'. I don't know why they wanted me."

Jim Beam, knew. He admired the certificate with its colored insignia and signatures from Dean Feldstein, Harry Lourie, the class academic coordinator and president of AOA. This was acknowledgement of her superior accomplishments.

"Well, I know, babe. I've known this all along. You're the best!" He was envious, wishing he had also received this honor … but, he was honest too. She deserved it. "Wow! I think you've done good, girl."

"Thanks," she smiled.

Jim had spent part of the evening at the library and had evidence to document his studying at attending rounds. He passed out stapled, Xeroxed papers among the team. "I've made copies of an article from the *Norwegian Archives of Medicine* on CPK-MB fragments. Since we used MB percentage to diagnose MIs, it is important to know the other sources of CPK-MB to avoid false positive diagnosis of MI, myocardial infarction. They studied fifty-eight mice and showed significant levels of MB in brain and, especially, kidney tissues. Most brain CPK is BB isozyme, but 2 percent is also MB. The renal CPK can be as high as 8 to 10 percent MB. Hence, patients with renal injury or disease might give us positive MBs on isozyme testing."

There was a pause as everyone glanced over the article. Dr. Strong cleared his throat and began a response. "Here is an interesting interaction between test-tube and clinical medicine. Even if we assume mouse kidney is representative of human tissue, the overwhelming majority of circulating CPK comes from MM components. This is due to the extremely large mass of skeletal muscle compared to the mass of brain or kidney. Other sources of CPK are only a fraction of total CPK and the portion of it that is attributable to kidney, brain, or heart is a fraction of a fraction. Even if a small percentage of renal CPK is MB, a large percentage of cardiac CPK is MB. I feel that this laboratory tidbit has little clinical significance in the diagnosis and management of suspected acute MI."

"… Unless you are a mouse," added Dr. Meriwether.

Obie was of the minority that retained his copy of the article after rounds. Medical students keep all printed matter they receive, afraid that a discarded piece of information would prove critical sometime in the future. He caught up to Jim.

"I enjoyed this article," he said. "I was a biochem major, and this stuff fascinates me."

"Yeah? Thanks, I guess. I'll be prepared if Mickey Mouse rolls in with chest pain."

Obie laughed at him.

Cheryl added from behind them, "Don't be silly, Jim. Mickey's not a veteran!"

"Hardy," beckoned Dr. Leming. "You done any intubations?"

"No, not yet."

"Come on! Strong says Mr. Ballister is pooping out. We're putting him on the vent." Dr. Leming assured Dr. Strong that "we" would get it done. "Since he's alert and still breathing on his own, we'll do a nasotracheal intubation." She concisely reviewed selecting endotracheal (ET) tube size, topical anesthesia to the nose, head positioning, and insertion technique. Hardy briefed the patient on what was happening while looking over the equipment Sara Leming had prepared.

Obie positioned himself to the right of Mr. Ballister, having selected the right-nostril side since it appeared more open. The patient was taking deep, quick breaths with prolonged exhaling. The clear plastic tube slid into the nose and down to above the larynx, steaming up rhythmically when the patient exhaled. This assured Obie he was near the trachea, above the vocal cords. He wanted to instruct the patient to take a deep breath, but feared the patient would reflexively tense up and impair the intubation. Obie hesitated, seemingly for minutes, matching the breathing rhythm. He then quickly shoved the tube in three or four inches further. The patient coughed with a little wheeze and then was silent, as the plastic tube held open his vocal cords. The exhalations fogged the tube more intensely, and a tubular, almost whistling, sound emitted from the nasal tube.

Quickly, Dr. Leming listened to the lungs and announced, "It's in! Good job! Now, *stat* portable chest X-ray and a ventilator!" She was inflating the balloon-cuff port to seal the tube in place.

Obie was pleased with the successful procedure, although he felt he had been extremely lucky. He was humbled, however, two days later when Dr. Strong held out the morning SMA-20 chemistry for him to see.

"See these labs?" he said. "When a patient is on the ventilator, everything must be done to build up his strength. This is necessary if we are ever going to wean him off respiratory support."

Obie glanced at Mr. Ballister's basic chemistries, but didn't see any alarming abnormalities in the electrolytes, kidney, or liver functions. Since he didn't respond promptly, Dr. Strong continued, "Did you see those phosphorous and magnesium levels? They were low yesterday too." Obie had ignored those little-used "mineral" levels on chemistries. "What are we going to do to fix these?"

Obie could not answer. These mineral problems were new and foreign to him. Dr. Strong interpreted his blank expression.

"All right," he said, a little disgusted. Obie followed him as he walked to the nurses' station and wrote an order in Mr. Ballister's chart, reading aloud as he wrote. "Give him one gram of magnesium sulfate daily, IV, over thirty minutes. And add fifteen milliequivalents of K-Phos per liter to his IV fluid." That was the extent of teaching Obie received from Dr. Strong. He was afraid to ask for elaboration, feeling guilt that his oversight had impeded Mr. Ballister's recovery.

Three days later, Obie gave his patient report during rounds. "Mr. Ballister was moved out of CCU yesterday, off the ventilator now after worsening emphysema. He is stable, but still having some tachycardia."

"Okay," approved Dr. Leming. "Next," she said as they continued around the ward. As Morningstar presented a heart-failure patient receiving aggressive diuretic therapy, she questioned, "When a patient is receiving high dose, multidrug therapy for diuresis, what things should we monitor?"

"Well," began Morningstar, "... other than weights and I and Os," he said, referring to intakes and outputs, "chemistries. Especially BUN, creatinine, and potassium."

"Anything else we might check?" No response arose. "Anyone?" Dr. Leming asked again as she looked over the group.

"Maybe magnesium," offered Obie.

"Excellent! Order a mag level with today's lab, Morningstar."

Christmas was Obie's night on call. He didn't want to neglect his responsibilities or appear weak by asking the resident physicians what he should do. At six a.m., he was retrieving labs and X-rays on his patients. He did take the liberty of riding his three-speed bicycle down the long corridor to radiology. He occasionally did this late at night when on call, when the halls were vacant, but was afraid to do it during the day. He was prepped with his index cards, lab results, and X-rays for rounds. Crystal Meriwether and Sara Leming arrived, along with Jim and Cheryl. Dr. Strong and

Morningstar were off duty.

"You students came in on Christmas?" asked Leming, incredulously. The students exchanged glances and looked back at Sara Leming.

"Well, I'm listed on call tonight," offered Obie.

"No one said anything about us being off," added Cheryl.

"Well, we're not having CCU rounds and presentations. We'll just do work rounds on the ward. Come on."

After rounds, she dismissed Jim and Cheryl, who happily left. Once they had gone, she spoke to Obie.

"Hardy, your rotation ends in three days. It's silly for you to pick up any new admissions on Christmas Day. Write your progress notes, check the new orders and labs, and then sign out to Meriwether."

"Okay, but I'd planned to stay for call."

"Yeah, I know. I'm going to be home with my pager on myself. Merry Christmas."

"Thanks! And Merry Christmas to you!"

It was almost noon when Obie biked into Dunston Manor Apartments. He wanted to surprise Priscilla, who had been waiting for him to call, hoping they could meet for lunch. They had planned to open their gifts on the twenty-sixth this year—a belated Christmas. When he opened the door, she looked puzzled. She was dressed, but still in her slippers.

"Merry Christmas, Prissy! I don't have to pull call tonight! I'm off!"

They hugged happily as Obie was so grateful to have worked only six hours on Christmas, instead of twenty-four.

Medicine, Team A, MCV West Hospital

Chapter 8
Medicine–West 15

O bie Hardy had ridden the MCV West Hospital elevators to the seventh floor, psychiatry, and eleventh floor, L&D, before but not as high as the fifteenth floor, general medicine. He stepped into the central hub and located the call room, the home base for his final medicine rotation—a new year, a new clinical rotation, a new medical team. The call room was tight quarters after the spacious VAH, but several times larger than that of L&D, and it had a small window. The view overlooked East Hospital and Church Hill.

The M-81 team included John Morgan and Barry Montgomery, with interns Crystal Meriwether from the last rotation on cardiology, and Stan Thurman. Barry was from Pennsylvania, slender at about six feet. His dirty blond hair was straight and short with stubby bangs that sat up. He leaned comfortably against the wall, holding a styrofoam cup of coffee. The JAR introduced himself as Dr. Skip Needleman and divided up the thirty-eight patients between the interns.

"Meriwether, you're on call tonight, so you get only sixteen patients. Thurman, you got twenty-two, but several are discharges for today and some easy cases. You studs can pick up two or three current patients and workup new admissions. You can work out a call schedule every third night amongst yourselves."

Dr. Harold Woodson was the attending. The medical team was hematology and oncology, but they took general medical admissions on rotation with the other services. Dr. Woodson was tall and elderly, probably in his late sixties. His features were exaggerated by age, the earlobes and nose particularly, and his dress a little baggy, giving him a cartoon-character appearance. Oncology was his specialty, and, despite his age and doted look, he was mentally sharp and intelligent.

After rounds, Skip Needleman assembled the group outside a patient's room.

"I'm going to in-service everyone on this new device. Patients requiring frequent IV chemo and even lab tests can have a permanent indwelling catheter put in. This new 'Hickman Catheter' tunnels under the skin, creating a biological barrier to bacteria. It can remain in place for months with much less risk of infection. Blood specimens can be obtained and medicine or blood transfusions given into a large central vein, usually subclavian. It does, however, require certain maintenance to prevent clotting and infections."

Mr. Sasser, victim of acute lymphocytic leukemia, ALL, had a Hickman catheter. He was average build, seventy-two years old, Caucasian, with somewhat tanned skin. Red and purple bruises were scattered over his upper extremities, telltale signs of a blood disorder. Dr. Needleman demonstrated the sterile technique when handling the white silicone catheter hub. He drew 10 cc of stagnant blood before collecting lab specimens and heparin anticoagulant flushes after each uncapping. He stressed the absolute necessity of maintaining sterility, avoiding the introduction of air into the catheter, and preventing clotting. Mr. Sasser smiled throughout the instructional session, content that the extra attention was to benefit his case.

The following morning, bright and early, John Morgan sat at the computer terminal in the call room, studying the green glowing digits on the screen. He held the light pen like a pencil in his right hand, its coiled cord trailing off to the rear of the monitor. After clicking the pen on the right targets on the screen, he would scribble notes onto his index cards. Each student had a unique identification code, allowing access to lab results, X-rays, and certain orders in the Hospital Information System, HIS. He cocked his head up as the intercom spoke.

"The Hospital Information System is down on level two. HIS is down on level two."

"What's level two?" asked Obie.

"I'm not sure," replied John. "There are different levels of access, like entering a new patient, entering orders, printing data, or just viewing information. Level zero means it is totally out, level four is the least interference."

The centralized computer system made viewing lab results and X-rays on patients efficient. There was difficulty, however, in accessing a free terminal at times. At change of shift, studs could utilize the nurses' station terminal while they were in report. On nights on call, it was easy to find free terminals. Each night from midnight to two a.m., unfortunately, HIS was down on level zero for maintenance. Despite the down times, it was a significant improvement over the mail-courier delivery at the VAH.

Barry Montgomery's bangs were disheveled the morning after call. He still sported a sleepy smile. His new admission report was concise, but fast-paced and to the point. Dr. Woodson was content with Barry's patient presentation, although Obie felt it was too cursory.

"Who has Mr. Parrish, hepatitis B?" asked Woodson.

"I do," answered Obie. "He's less jaundiced, is eating, and his temperature is 99.1."

"Good, what are his enzymes today?"

"I don't know, sir. Yesterday the SGOT was …"

"Yesterday?" interrupted Woodson. "Yesterday? You don't know your patient's current liver enzymes?"

"Ah … no, sir. Not today's labs."

"And what is his diagnosis?"

"Hepatitis B," replied Obie weakly. Dr. Woodson silently stared at Obie for an eternal thirty seconds.

"You students have only a few patients each. There is no reason for anyone to not know *all* their labs, test results, and vital signs. This won't happen again … Get me those results."

Obie obeyed, slinking out of the room, having failed his duty. He had felt that having enzymes done everyday was superfluous. The SGOT had been 1,400 and was now below 800, on an improving trend the past three days. Whether the level fell by 210 points or 360 points seemed to be irrelevant. Mr. Parrish was clinically improving—wasn't that the important thing?

After rounds, as they left the residents' room, Barry leaned over to Obie. "We need some bean."

"Bean?" queried Obie.

Barry tapped his empty styrofoam cup and repeated, "Bean."

"Coffee! … Yeah!"

"Ca'mahwn, " motioned Barry. He led Obie to the nurses lounge. "They don't mind, if we contribute to the fund." He dropped a quarter into the canister labeled "coffee money" and poured each of them a cup. Obie deposited an equivalent donation. "Ten minutes at the computer before rounds, and you can have *all* your patients' labs. You need 'flea food' for rounds."

"Thanks, Barry. And … thanks for the 'bean,' too!"

Obie was pulling call with Crystal Meriwether. He studied her short, straight auburn hair as he stood behind her. She was fairly attractive, medium build, about five foot tall, and perky and smart. Her white lab coat sported the green MCV monogram patch on the shoulder. She was wearing the institution-issued white pants with a button-up flowered blouse.

"It's easier to read these when they're positive," she stated, not looking up from the binocular microscope in the lab. The oil emersion objective lens provided the maximum magnification, 1000 X, routinely achieved with a light microscope. "When you see AFBs, you're done. If you don't see them, you have to keep looking until you're sure." AFBs—acid fast bacilli—usually meant TB. They had just prepared several of the specialized stains of sputum spread thinly on a glass slide. A newly admitted pneumonia patient was the source. "Well, you can try a while," she offered to Obie, surrendering her stool. "I'm going to finish my write-up."

Obie lasted only five minutes scanning the smear, feeling motion sickness as the magnified viewing field rolled side to side and up and down.

"Negative for AFBs," he concluded.

Ellen Partridge was on obese lady who suffered from ITP, idiopathic thrombocytopenia purpura. She required IV steroids to suppress the immunological destruction of her platelets, the blood elements used in clotting. Her IV was out, and the midnight dose was due.

"Hardy," asked Meriwether, "I've got another admission in the ER. Can you restart Partridge's IV while I go downstairs?"

"Sure, " he replied. This was a chance to impress the intern with his clinical skills. His eagerness, however, was short-lived. Ms. Partridge's fat forearms were edematous, worsened by the IV fluids and the methylprednisolone infusions. Even though her skin was dark brown, it was peppered with purplish-red splotches. He didn't find the engorged veins he desired after tying the rubber tourniquet around first one arm, and then the other. He first tried a tiny vein on the back of the hand. A purplish bruise appeared after a little probing, signaling a doomed attempt. *Well,* he thought, *that was a twenty-gauge ... Maybe ... a twenty-two would go in.* He walked to the supply room for another twenty- and twenty-two-gauge needle. The opposite hand was also unsuccessful, and a third attempt was in the forearm. He wiped alcohol over the skin, patted the surface, and adjusted the gooseneck lamp to eliminate glare. Maybe this would be the vein.

"I'm sorry, Ms. Partridge. I'll try my best to get it this time. If I'm not lucky, I'll quit."

A slow needle penetration of the skin is more painful. This attempt was slow.Ms. Partridge whimpered and inhaled loudly through her teeth. A drop of blood appeared in the needle hub! Obie hooked up the IV fluid and opened the clamped valve. Her skin began to swell around the needle site. Obie was sickened.

"I'm so sorry, Ms. Partridge. It won't run. I'm stopping now. You can rest." Obie gathered the wrappers, cotton balls, and needles and retreated. Mere disappointment was not what he felt—more like total worthlessness.

"Oh, you got Ms. Partridge's IV in. Good!" said the nurse he met at the supply room.

"No. I wasn't lucky," he replied.

"Not 'lucky'? How am I going to give her her steroids? Her platelet count's only 16,000!"

"Well … Dr. Meriwether …"

"Dr. Meriwether? Dr. Meriwether might be hours getting back up here!"

"Okay, I'll look again," he said. Platelet counts are usually in the 200,000 range. The 16,000 sounded critically low. He had told the patient he was stopping after his three failed attempts; now he would be asking her to bare her arms again for more stabbing. Gathering up more gauze pads, alcohol wipes, and Jelco needles, Obie again, reluctantly, entered Ms. Partridge's room.

"Ms. Partridge, I'm sorry but you *have* to get your medication. I've got to start this IV on you now."

"I figured as much," she replied.

Obie again tightened the pale gold rubber tourniquet around Ms. Partridge's left arm and repeated his exam of her forearm. His confidence was at its nadir, his patience short, and his fifth assault on her vascular was unsuccessful. He stood up, looked toward the door, and the thought of fleeing the room welled up in his chest. Before his feet could take flight, he took a deep breath, slowly exhaling, trying to release the frustration and sense of failure from his body.

No, he thought, *There's no one else to do this. Her health is dependent on this procedure. You* cannot *accept failure.*

"I'm sorry," he said as he moved to the other side of the bed. He tied the tourniquet up high on her arm, right at the armpit. Massaging and stroking the entire upper limb, Obie searched for signs of veins. He placed the bedside gooseneck light to shine across her arm at an angle, intensifying shadows and skin-surface irregularities. A tiny dark pattern appeared on the inner side of her arm, above the elbow. Obie told himself, "Okay. Here's a vein. I'll just start a routine IV in it. Just a typical IV like I start everyday." He did select the smaller, twenty-two-gauge Jelco needle; routine alcohol prep done; skin dried; IV fluid ready; and the tubing flushed with fluid, primed.

"Yes!" he exclaimed as the flash of blood filled the hub of the Jelco. He attached the tubing and opened the valve; it flowed perfectly. "We got it!" he announced to a relieved Ms. Partridge.

At morning rounds, Dr. Montgomery asked of Dr. Meriwether, "And what's Ms. Partridge's platelet count today?"

"It's up to 48. She's on IV Solumedrol."

Obie felt the warmth of self-satisfaction, knowing his role in the "IV" drugs. The steroids were working!

"Good. I think we can switch her to prednisone tablets now. She shouldn't need anymore IV steroids."

The fruits of Obie's labors were spoiled now—the IV becoming unnecessary only eight hours later.

"Mr. Sasser, the ALL patient, how is he doing?" he continued.

"His blood cultures are growing yeast, Candida albicans. Maybe that's what's causing his fever and sweats. Not just the cancer," responded Obie.

"So what do we treat this with?"

Obie could only relate the yeast infections from GYN rotation.

"Nystatin?" he guessed.

"No, he needs more intensive treatment. Systemic, IV anti-fungals. Amphotericin."

"We call it 'ampho-terrible,'" elaborated Dr. Needleman later in the elevator, "since it has so many toxicities and side effects. It affects almost every organ system: brain, lung, heart, liver, kidney, and blood systems."

The doors opened at basement level, and the team exited, continuing to the radiology reading room. Dr. Needleman had requested West 15's patients' films for review. The radiologist had them ready to view.

"Lavern Allison, who had her?" Needleman began.

"I do," chirped John Morgan. "She's the one …"

"Ah-ah-ot," interrupted Needleman. "Hardy, what do you see here?"

Obie leaned forward, and then stepped back to get a full perspective.

"We-be," whispered Barry in Obie's direction.

"Well,…" he began, "there are some densities in the center part. The hilums … *hila*. Doesn't look like pneumonia."

"Perihilar adenopathy," announced the radiologist. "Common causes?"

"Lymphoma?" offered Obie.

"We-be," Barry softly hinted again.

"Right," the radiologist said. "Or in a young black female, like this?"

"Sarcoidosis?"

"That's it! Classic findings."

John grinned and rubbed under his chin. Barry smirked and acknowledged the correct diagnosis, "Ca'mahwn!"

The radiologist walked them through the proper way to approach chest-X-ray interpretation. First look at the background structures such as spine, shoulders, and ribs, and then the clinically relevant heart shadow and lungs. "Now, using this technique, look at this film and tell me what's unusual."

John pressed closest to the film, studying it intensely. "Well," he began, "the bone structure and breast shadows look like a young adult female. The lung pattern looks like congestive heart failure ... but the heart is not enlarged."

"Exactly! Why is this unusual?"

"Because CHF is usually seen in old folks," stated Barry.

"Yes. This pulmonary edema is from a narcotic overdose. I think she may be one of your classmates."

John put his finger on the name-imprint space and Obie could read "Newman, Kathy." There was also the image of an endotracheal tube, indicating that she was on a respirator, critical condition. The studs exchanged concerned glances. Kathy might not be all right after all. Narcotics carry immediate dangers for patients but additionally jeopardize any career in health care.

They were quiet while returning to the W 15 call room. Obie broke the somber silence, "Barry, what was that 'we-be' stuff you were whispering?"

"'We-bes.' You know, black people. They get sarcoidosis."

"Oh ... but 'we-be'?"

"You know, like when they say 'We-be going to the sto' now.'"

"Yeah, I see," Obie, acknowledging this cryptic euphemism for blacks. The proper term for referring to their race had evolved, every appropriate term falling into disfavor by the members of the race when they adopted each new designation. Using an outdated reference then became offensive to members of the race. Evolution from "nigger" to "Negro" to "colored people" to "people of color" and now "black" had progressed. "We-be" seemed to bypass the system, hence not being outwardly offensive.

The M-81s dispersed to do their daily scut work—Obie to Mr. Sasser's room. He was careful as he collected a blood culture from the Hickman catheter, maintaining sterile technique. Another fever spike prompted another infectious workup. A second culture from a peripheral, arm vein would also be needed.

"How do you feel, Mr. Sasser?" queried Obie, trying to distract him from the needle stick in his arm.

"Honestly? Like crap!" He was now speckled with red, purple, and blue dots and splotches over his body. His lips were cracked with dried blood that formed a sticky crust along their edges. He looked like crap too.

"You didn't have relatives with leukemia, did you?" asked Obie.

"No, ... but my hobby is refinishing furniture. Some doctors think that exposure to the fumes and chemicals in the paint strippers and thinners over a period of time could cause cancers."

"That's a bummer," Obie noted. "We hope this fungal infection will respond to the Amph-a-terrib ... I mean, Amphotericin."

Mr. Sasser did not improve. Blood and platelet transfusions were needed over the next few days. He was losing weight, his appetite was failing, and he was running fevers. Obie admired his strained smile and the life in his eyes—a spark of hope despite his declining course. He was appreciative of his care. Something about him had seemed familiar to Obie. Sasser? ... Yes! One of the leukemia samples he tested during his research project had been "Sasser." It was this same, kind man.

Dr. Woodson commented during rounds, "Mr. Sasser has failed to achieve remission. Our therapy from this point on is only supportive care." Obie suspected this, but was saddened to hear it stated officially. He yearned to have something else to offer Mr. Sasser. He wished that his research project could have helped him. After rounds, his heavy mood was interrupted by Dr. Meriwether.

Crystal Meriwether announced, "Obie, you get the Mellette patient on 16. This is Dr. Mellette's private patient. We'll do the medical care, but Woodson won't be the attending we report to."

"Okay. The patient's on 16?"

"West 16, one floor up. It's the 'private' floor."

Obie had never been to West 16, assuming it was a non-patient care floor. The rooms were spacious, neat and new looking. Each was a private room too. There was a rooftop solarium on the south end overlooking Broad Street and, further south, the James River. It was quiet, no bustling of med students and teams of doctors.

Betty Oakley was in room 18—a breast cancer patient. She had completed radiation and two courses of chemo but continued to decline. She was wasted, cachectic, and dehydrated. Obie was afraid to touch her, fearful that he would hurt or bruise her. He limited his student exam and got most of her medical history from the old chart.

"I talked to Mellette," Dr. Meriwether said. "Ms. Oakley is terminal, end stage. We are to provide comfort care measures only … And, she's a 'No Code'." That meant no resuscitation measures.

"Good," he replied. "I felt like I would break her just examining her."

Obie was describing West 16 to the other M-81s. John Morgan was nodding approvingly.

"Yeah," John stated, always a step ahead of everyone. "I have a patient up there too. The chief. It's kinda neat to eat lunch on the roof there when it's sunny."

That night on call, Obie was paired with intern Stan Thurman. Obie fielded the calls on Ms. Oakley, since she was his and Dr. Meriwether's patient. The nursing staff called every hour for pain medication or low blood pressure readings or pauses in her respirations. She was given morphine, boluses of IV fluids, oxygen, and blood-pressure medications in IV drips. Her urine output decreased; a diuretic was given. Her blood pressure would then drop. Obie was in and out of her room during the following day, anticipating her demise at any time. She lingered still.

At 5:30 p.m., his thirty-sixth hour on duty, Obie was again at her bedside. Her respirations were erratic with intermittent pauses. She was dusky in color and clammy to touch. He was tired, frustrated, and sad. Would the attending physician think Ms. Oakley received inadequate care? Could anything else be done?

An elderly woman entered the room. Her hair was blond and gray, a soothing smile was on her face, and her eyes twinkled. Obie recognized her, remembering his med school interview with Dr. Mellette. They had discussed the college theater and travel experiences during his interview. It had been a refreshing change from the academic drilling of Med-CATS exam scores and grade-point averages. She had a comforting, maternal air about her.

"Hardy?" she queried.

"Yes, ma'am. Dr. Mellette."

"You had any time for plays recently?"

Obie was amazed. Did she recall his interview from over three years ago? "No, not hardly," he responded.

They turned to Ms. Oakley, and Dr. Mellette gently held her hand. "It's Dr. Mellette, Betty. Everything's okay."

Ms. Oakley's eyes opened very slightly, turned toward the voice, and then closed. She took a slow breath and paused, followed by a second, slower breath. Her breathing stopped. She looked peaceful as she died holding the hand of this incredible physician. Had she been lingering all this time, waiting for Dr. Mellette's blessing to leave this world? Dr. Mellette held her hand a few minutes in silence, Obie watching in awe. She turned to Obie, her smile now saddened but enduring.

"Thank you for all your help, Hardy." His efforts now seemed justified. How often in the twentieth century does someone die holding the hand of their personal physician?

"Sure. It's still sad, though," he answered.

"Her suffering and fighting are over. Now she can rest." Dr. Mellette patted Obie on the shoulder as they left the room.

Obie was vacuous on his bike ride home, to the COOP. The COOP was a large farmhouse on Creighton Road, the farm having become a nursery. He shared the house with three fourth-year medical students, M-80s, and a dental student. The bank had printed the house expense account statement—"Creighton Co-

Op"— as the "Creighton Coop." It seemed right somehow. The winter night was dark, cold, and empty. The fatigue of thirty-six hours on call, the shock of a classmate's overdose, and the death of a patient had drained Obie of energy and feelings. There were no more streetlights on Creighton Road the last three-quarters of a mile to Glenside Nursery. Turning down the gravel drive, his face was numb from the cold, and his hands were stiffly gripping the handlebars. As he circled to the back, in the backdoor light he saw the shadowy shape of a blue Sunbird. As Obie closed the back door, Priscilla walked into the kitchen from inside. He embraced her and suddenly was hungry, smelling an aroma in the air.

"I stopped by Jerry's Pizza on the way over," she said, smiling and opening the oven. "Medium Italian sausage." She pulled the pizza box from the warm oven and produced a Michelob Light from the refrigerator.

"Wow!" exclaimed Obie, his body's frigid shell beginning to warm. "This is really great, Priss. Thanks."

"You can make it up to me tomorrow," she said. "You'll be worthless tonight."

Priscilla was replenishing the vitality the past thirty-six hours had drained from Obie. He loved her for this, flooding him with positive nutrients when his entire psyche was depleted. She spent the night at the COOP, squeezed into Obie's twin-sized bed with him. He slept.

The Creighton COOP, Hardy's place 1980

The next morning, she drove him to work, and he was physically and emotionally recharged, able to plunge into another day of medicine. After rounds, Obie shared the Dr. Mellette story with his peers.

"The Chief's dying too," reported John. "He's a Pamunkey Indian, a tribal elder ... I think a chief. I've been following him on West 16. He has lung cancer. Too much peace pipe, I guess. The tribe doesn't completely embrace modern medicine, not wishing to discredit their medicine men. He wants to live as long as possible but not compromise their culture. Hard decisions for a leader."

"Ca'mahwn," commented Barry, holding up his cup of bean. "All I got is a 'we-be' with sickle cell."

"You heard anymore about Kathy Newman?" asked Obie.

"I heard she's better, probably being released today," said John. "I'm sure she'll have to repeat third year completely ... if they don't drop her."

"It's such a waste," said Obie.

Obie's next call night was fairly quiet; he finished an admission and the ward's scut work before midnight. He found a bunk in the call room and laid down for a nap. At one thirty a.m. he was awakened to bells ringing and flashing lights. He bolted out to the nurses' station to find out what was happening.

"It's the fire alarm," stated the nurse matter-of-factly. "Probably just a cigarette in a waste can or something."

"How do you shut it off?" he asked.

"Can't. Only the firemen can shut it off. They have to respond to every call."

Obie heard the fire-truck sirens and horn-honking from the street fifteen stories below as the ringing pulsations continued. The high-pitched sounds penetrated his body, causing an overall irritation. After thirty minutes, the firemen finally silenced the alarm and deemed the floor secure. Obie returned to his bunk and was almost on the verge of sleep when he was jarred awake again.

"Mr. Winn has a BP of 84/40!" exclaimed the nurse who had previously told him about the fire alarm. Obie went to Mr. Winn's room, took another BP reading, and got 104/62 with a normal pulse rate. He reviewed the chart, finding his routine BP readings to range 98 to 115 on the upper, systolic, numbers. Convinced that this was Mr. Winn's usual two-thirty-a.m. blood pressure, he retreated again to the bunk. Obie closed his eyes.

"The Hospital Information System is down on level zero. HIS is down on level zero," blared the intercom system. Obie rolled over, as if he could erase the disturbance by a new body position. Unsuccessful in his sleep efforts, he sat up, groggy, trying to form a plan that would prepare himself ahead of time for rounds. He couldn't check labs since HIS was down. It was too early to examine his patients, although he guessed they had not slept all too well either. He was debating on finding a cup of bean when the all-too-familiar night nurse tapped on the call room door.

"Mr. Sasser has expired," she quietly stated.

Nassawaddox Accomack Memorial (NAM) Hospital, 1980

Chapter 9
Community Medicine

The explosion of knowledge in the twentieth century led to increased specialization of physicians. More fields of specialization emerged, and even the GPs, general practitioners, spawned the specialty of "family practice," or FP. MCV strived to promote these specialties, establishing a four week clinical rotation of community medicine. These rotations placed the M-81s in various communities across Virginia, especially in the MCV FP training program sites in Virginia Beach, Newport News, Blackstone, and Chesterfield. Students had an opportunity to request their preferences for consideration in placement, but places in certain sites were mandatory. At their community medicine orientation, they received their assignments.

Dr. Fitzhugh Mayo was a tall man with wavy black hair. He had a prominent square jaw and broad shoulders. His private practice in Virginia Beach had become a MCV FP residency through his pioneering efforts. He was head of the community medicine program and addressed the M-81s at the orientation.

"The rotation sites outside of Richmond have lodging facilities for you. You will need to provide your own meals, however. These sites are real practices; many are indeed private practices. You will be representing your school and your medical student class. Please remember that you are guests, and be courteous. You will have an opportunity to make your comments when you turn in your rotation evaluations."

Dean Feldstein was quiet and solemn, looking down through his black-rimmed glasses. Kathy Newman sat across from his desk, her makeup not concealing the rings under her eyes. Her face was drawn, and her eyes were sunken and glazed.

"Kathy, you know my daughter, Martha Rae, is in your class. She was an M-80, but she didn't pass the national board exam. She repeated second year. I've given you more favors than I gave my own daughter. This will be the last," he said.

"Yes, sir. Thank you for your help," she answered.

"You keep clean, attend the counseling and the random drug screens; and if—*if*—everything is 100 percent, you can retake your third year. Understand?"

"Yes, sir. I'm so grateful for your help. I won't let you down again, you'll see."

"All right then. And good luck."

Obie had requested Nassawadox, on the eastern shore, and was matched to that site. As he drove his Chevette east of Norfolk, he remembered his first trip across the Chesapeake Bay Bridge Tunnel on a college road trip to Ocean City, Maryland. Driving down from the elevated bridge approaching the east end gave a clear, panoramic view of Fisherman's Isle. The afternoon sun made the white sand gleam, contrasting against the vivid blue water. The island remained untouched by human development—no buildings or power lines. Its natural beauty was beckoning, even in mid-winter.

The drive up Route 13 was scenic, with vast acres of harvested peanuts, corn, and grains that awaited the spring cultivation. The highway was fairly flat and straight, welcoming sightseeing along the drive. Abandoned farmhouses still stood amid the fields, souvenirs of a plantation family lifestyle. Northampton-Accomack Memorial Hospital, known as NAM, was in Nassawadox, visible to the left of Route 13 North, standing three stories high. NAM Hospital was a 115-bed facility built in 1971, replacing the smaller 1928 structure. The original hospital initially took eight years to fund and build, overlapping the Great Depression era. It resulted from a true, grass-roots community effort as area residents were urged to "donate a day's wages" to support their hospital. Some of the donations were just one dollar, as farmers and watermen were the predominant "industry".

Obie reported to the front desk and was escorted by the nursing supervisor to the students' quarters off of the second floor. It was an apartment like area with three bedrooms, each with bunk beds, and a kitchen and den area. Cindy Weston had already arrived and, as the only female, had claimed a bedroom of her own. She introduced Obie to Al Fowler, a student from Eastern Virginia Medical School in Norfolk. He was tall, but not muscular—a bit on the flabby side. Al had large glasses and, with his long face, reminded Obie of an owl. He had been there two weeks already and had one more week to complete. Obie took the last bedroom and unpacked his Lange series textbook *Current Medical Therapy 1979* and *The Washington Manual*. He placed a photo of Priscilla bedside the books on the dormitory-type desk.

Robert Hammer was the last M-81 to arrive, around ten o'clock at night. He had light brown hair, a short-trimmed beard, and smelled of cigarette smoke. Obie directed him to the empty top bunk in his room. Placing his duffle bag bedside the bunks, Robert opened it to produce a six pack of Natural Light beer. Obie noted that a corner of the cardboard carton had been torn and a bottle was missing. Robert freed another two bottles and handed one to Obie, smiling friendly. They sat out in the lounge area and talked about college and medical school, unwinding from their drives.

Al Fowler came out of his room, and Obie introduced him to Robert, who offered him a beer as well.

"No thanks," he responded politely. "Oh, and in case you haven't read through the hospital's policies," he said, pointing to the pamphlet on the kitchen counter, "it's against the rules to have alcohol or to smoke inside the hospital." He smiled, a bit smugly, and walked back toward his room. "Good night. I'll see you guys tomorrow."

"Good night ... and thanks!" responded Robert. He and Obie looked at each other, each holding a bottle of contraband. Robert held up his bottle and grinned, "To community medicine!"

"Here, here! To community medicine!" responded Obie, clicking his bottle against Robert's.

"And to MCV," added Robert, nodding to Al Fowler's room.

The first morning, they met their preceptors in the hospital lobby at seven thirty for rounds. Robert was paired with Dr. William Benart, an FP, and Cindy with his partner, Dr. Dixon. Obie was to work under Dr. Drury Stith, hematologist-oncologist. Dr. Stith was tall, about six foot two, with a light brown mustache. He was medium build and wore a dress shirt with a button-down collar and no tie. He led Obie into the doctors' lounge and showed him the EKG box where the tracings were placed for interpretation.

"If you get bored or industrious, come down here and read my EKGs. Just paperclip your reading to it, since I have to sign 'em off anyway," Dr. Stith explained. "Here's our census sheet. My patients are listed with my name beside 'em." He handed Obie a computer-printout sheet. "We round about seven thirty each day and start at the office at nine. Where you from?" he continued as they walked off to the right of the lobby.

"Boydton, Virginia. A rural town—smaller than Nassawadox."

"Smaller than this? That's hard to imagine," he said as they entered the glass doors to the ICU. He pointed to the "Room" column on Obie's census sheet. "The ICU patients have zeros in front of their numbers. I've got three in here now. First is Ms. Dise, pulmonary embolus, on a heparin drip. What should her PTT level be?"

"Ah … 60 to 70?" guessed Obie.

"That's right! You've done your medicine rotations already?"

"Yeah. And psych and OB."

"Good! You'll actually be some help to me this month."

They continued through the ICU and the two floors, and headed over to the office. The building was a two-story brick complex with multiple physicians' offices. It was a block across from the front of the hospital. In the back of the doctors' offices was a lounge area with an adjacent conference room. Dr. Stith invited Obie to read in his office between patients and when he was seeing patients who preferred not to have medical students present. His receptionist stepped in and handed him a chart.

"Dr. Stith, Mr. Throckmorton is on the phone about his excision."

"Okay, sure," he said and picked up the receiver. "Mr. Throckmorton? … Yeah. I got back the report. It was cancer … Sure thing … Okay, you're welcome. Take care now."

"You just tell people over the phone that they have *cancer*?" asked Obie unbelievingly. He imagined the drama, like a TV soap opera, of gathering the family in the doctor's office to receive the news.

"Oh, it's just a skin cancer. The watermen here are used to it. Very common. They're considered an occupational hazard."

On Wednesday afternoon, Dr. Benart assembled the students in the conference room for a lecture. He was middle-aged with a receding hairline, and was dark complexioned and intellectually sharp.

"Medical school teaches you science and disease management. It fails, however, to prepare you for private practice—the business of practicing medicine. I have some tidbits of advice that may be useful in setting yourselves up.

"Wherever you go, you first need to find a place to live and a place to work. You can buy or lease, but initially, find these buildings."

As he elaborated, Obie wrote a note: "#1—Cover your head."

"The second thing you need to have is insurance. You'll need medical liability or malpractice, life, and health insurance for yourself. You can't risk losing everything suddenly."

Obie continued his notes: "#2—Cover your ass."

Dr. Benart detailed these suggestions with scenarios and examples. "Once these are in place, you need to organize your business. You should seek out experts for this: an accountant, a lawyer, a banker, and so forth."

Obie's last entry: "#3—Take care of business."

Back in the students' apartment, Robert gave his opinion of the lecture, "That wasn't all that useful to me. I'm on an Air Force scholarship. I'll just be working for Uncle Sam."

"I dunno," stated Cindy. "We don't get information like that at MCV. It might prove quite useful one day."

"I took some notes," added Obie.

This was the earliest day yet that they had finished up. The short winter days made daylight precious. Obie changed to go running before it got completely dark. He liked to run around when visiting a new area to get oriented—a ground-level view of the roads. He ran south from the hospital and turned right on the first road headed west, toward the sun as it inched toward the horizon. The air was cold and dry, and Obie clenched his fists tightly to keep his hands warm. There was a white, clapboard-sided building on the back road with a sign saying "Town Hall." Obie marveled that it appeared one-room, the size of a large shed or a small garage. He tried to picture a council meeting or a local election in such a small place. There wasn't an outhouse, so there must be a bathroom crammed inside as well, if it had any plumbing at all. As the dusk light faded, the hospital lights were a welcome sight as he finished his frigid, perspiration-free run. He found the route he had wanted to find leading west to the Chesapeake Bay—for driving on later.

Thursday, Dr. Stith returned to the hospital at lunch time for an admission. Mr. Perdue appeared ill, his skin a sickly yellow color and his abdomen bloated. He was complaining of pain and constipation for eight days. After a brief exam, Dr. Stith retreated to the nurses' station and opened the chart.

"He has end-stage pancreatic cancer. I've been seeing him with Dr. McIntyre. We can only offer him comfort care at this point," Dr. Stith explained. "I asked him what he wanted the most and he said a beer."

"Not very good for his liver," noted Obie.

"Doesn't matter at this point. He probably has days to a week or two to live. If he'll enjoy a beer, why not?" Obie watched as Dr. Stith wrote in the hospital orders, "Give one beer per day."

"Does the hospital have beer?" asked Obie, remembering the policy brochure.

"They'll get it. I'm writing for a pain 'cocktail', too. I use a mixture of narcotics and sedatives, such as: morphine, Tylenol, hydroxyzine, and valium. The hydroxyzine helps with the nausea and the valium gives them a little bit of a buzz." Obie was accustomed to the MCV standard of fighting for every minute of life, performing code-blue resuscitations on terminal patients. Accepting death was a fresh approach, and it even addressed it with some dignity. He now realized that Dr. Stith had a high CQ.

After finishing the office later, Obie returned to the nurses' station on the second floor.

"Did anyone get Mr. Perdue's beer?" he asked the unit clerk.

"No," she answered. "The kitchen didn't have any, so we're going to have the nursing supervisor go get some."

"Hold off a minute," said Obie. "I'll be right back." He returned in two minutes with a cold Natural Light. "Here. He can have this," offered Obie. "I'll keep some on hand for him as long as he wants it."

Al Fowler opened the refrigerator in the students' dormitory. "Hey! There's a six pack of Michelob Lite in here."

"It's okay," responded Obie. "Dr. Stith needs some beer for a terminal patient." Al Fowler studied Obie's face, realizing this could be true and legit. "I'm sure he won't miss one occasionally. Help yourself."

Al pondered this briefly, and then reached for one of the brown bottles. "All right, then. Thanks!"

"So, what's the weekend looking like?" continued Obie.

"I'm going to head back to Norfolk. Being gone for a month gets hectic. I need to check up on some things. The bridge-tunnel's too expensive to go back every weekend."

Robert emerged from the bunk room, freshly showered and dressed.

"Where ya headed?" asked Obie.

"Oh, I'm going to look for a bar or something," he answered.

"Good luck!" Al said. "There's a bar in Accomack, about seventeen miles north. But the pizza place in Exmore serves beer."

"Pizza sounds good," said Obie.

"All right. You guys coming?" continued Robert.

"Sure," joined Al.

"Cindy, you want to go out with us for pizza?" called Robert toward the other bunk room.

"Yeah, sure."

Nelson's Pizza was about a mile north of the hospital. It was a versatile establishment, with a projection TV boasting a thirty-six-inch-high screen as well as a side room with two pool tables. The studs sat at a round table sharing a large pizza—half deluxe and half pepperoni. A basketball game was playing on TV.

"Dr. Benart complains about the UVA warm-up suits," said Bob. "The state emblem doesn't include the Eastern Shore of

Virginia. He's thinking of changing his support to the University of Maryland."

"He's right, though," said Obie. "I'd never noticed that before."

"What do you think of the two locals near the TV?" asked Bob. He nodded toward a table with two young girls, one black haired and the other with honey brown curls.

"They're not my type," said Cindy.

"I don't know," said Obie. "Their friends may be the ones playing pool. I think I'd watch them a bit first."

"I'm going to try to talk to the light-haired one," said Bob, taking his beer mug and standing up. Obie, being from a small town, respected the community bond that the Nassawadoxuns might have and the personal space with which they distanced themselves from strangers. Bob approached the table and began talking. After a short time, the black-haired girl arose and headed to the restroom. Seizing the opportunity, Bob sat down at the table with honey-hair and continued to talk. When the other of the pair emerged from the ladies room, she paused briefly, seeing Bob seated at her table, and then walked over to the pool tables. A couple of young men were playing a game of pool, and her arrival caused a pause. She spoke to the man in a black-and-red-plaid-flannel shirt and jeans, who looked over at the table. He started walking toward Bob and the light-haired girl, carrying his cue stick. As the guy approached, he flipped the pool stick backward and began pounding the butt of the stick into his left palm. Bob sat with his back toward the man, writing a note on a napkin.

Obie could feel the tension in his body as the impending conflict grew nearer. Bob was going to need his help fighting off the pool man. Al couldn't be depended upon as an ally in a brawl. Obie felt his pants to assure himself that he had his pocket knife with him.

Bob stood up and nodded to the girl, smiling, as the pool man arrived. The girl stood and introduced the men, with Bob smiling and extending his hand. The pool man did not smile, but he did nod ever so slightly, stance squared, maintaining a tight grip on his cue stick.

"Well?" Cindy asked Bob as he reclaimed his seat at the round table.

"She is here with some friends," he explained. "But she gave me the name of her cousin who works in the ER," he continued, waving the napkin he had written on.

Friday afternoon, Bob left for his date with the ER nurse, and Al left for Norfolk. Since they were spending the weekend at NAM Hospital, Obie and Cindy reported for Saturday rounds with the attendings. Dr. McIntyre was on call and rounded on all the patients for their group. As they finished ICU rounds, Dr. McIntyre led them to the ER for a new admission. The man was comatose and breathing rapidly.

"Brainstem, pontine, stroke," explained McIntyre. "This is usually seen in patients with very high blood pressures." He pointed to the ER chart, showing a BP of 178/110. "We use heparin for ischemic or embolic strokes, but this is probably hemorrhagic—an acute bleeding. Blood thinners like heparin would worsen it, although his prognosis is grim anyway."

While Dr. McIntyre wrote his admission orders, Obie and Cindy checked the physical findings.

"You may find his brainstem reflexes affected," offered McIntyre. "Try the cold water calorics. Squirt some ice water in his ear. If the brainstem is out, you'll get no corrective response. Normally, the eyes deviate to the side but jerk back, trying to maintain gaze. Remember 'COWS'? 'Cold Opposite, Warm Same' for the eye movements?"

"Yeah," replied Obie, remembering this obscure test from neurology. He got some cold water from the fountain, and Cindy dribbled it into the patients ears. No eye movements occurred.

"Neat!" said Cindy.

After rounds and a brief jog, Obie drove around with Cindy. He showed her the "Town Hall" and the dock at Bayford, a few miles west. They had beer and sub sandwiches at Nelson's Pizza afterwards. Cindy shared her idea of becoming an anesthesiologist. Her patients would be asleep, and she wouldn't have to do patient care, H&Ps, and rounds. Obie told of his desire to do rural family practice, although his volunteer-rescue-squad work during college still made emergency medicine appealing. They decided to take a road trip Sunday.

Bob joined them Sunday for an excursion to Assateague Island, a national park about forty-five miles north at the Maryland border. The Eastern Shore is also called the Del-Mar-Va Peninsula since it is composed of portions of Delaware, Maryland, and Virginia. At Chincoteague, they turned left to enter the island park. The Assateague Island National Seashore Park is on a thirty-seven-mile island that extends into Maryland. It is a popular haven for migratory birds.

The Canadian geese looked graceful with their long necks and black-trimmed beaks. The male mallards stood out, boasting their deep green heads and white-ringed necks. Obie, Cindy, and Bob walked over to the water's edge for closer looks, and the birds, though wild, would not swim off. They were somewhat tolerant of humans, as long as they could enjoy the amenities of the refuge. Seagulls and terns were also well represented. The closer look excursions from the car were often brief, cut short by blasts of February wind through the twenty-two-degree air.

Obie met Dr. Stith at seven thirty Monday for rounds. Their usual inpatient load of ten to twelve patients was down to six. The brainstem stroke patient and Mr. Perdue, the pancreatic cancer patient, were no longer on the census list.

"The Grim Reaper struck this weekend," stated Dr. Stith, musing a little, trying to lighten the burden of three weekend deaths. "They were only suffering, anyway. It's better that they didn't linger in misery."

"Oh, man. I kind of liked Mr. Perdue," responded Obie sincerely.

"Yeah. There's no effective treatment for pancreatic cancer, and the twelve-month survival rate is only 10 percent. It's also a painful course."

As he scanned the census sheet, Obie remembered a question he had pondered before. "Dr. Stith, why do some patients have a comma after their last name and some have a semicolon? Are all these typos?"

"Well, it's administrative. To get federal and public funding, we have to report usage by blacks and minorities. It's illegal, however, under equal rights to list racial information. Hence, the blacks are tabulated by using the semicolons."

"Okay," said Obie, thinking *the 'we-bes' here are the 'semicolons'.*

One of the advantages of community medicine at NAM was the free meals. Obie loved the congealed salads. He was eating a raspberry gelatin square with layers of cream cheese, whipped cream, and pecans. Cindy sat across the cafeteria table from him.

"What do you have planned this weekend?" Cindy asked.

"Priscilla, my girlfriend, is driving up Saturday morning. We'll probably get a motel room Saturday night."

"In Nassawadox?"

"Well, there's the Candlelight Inn a few miles south on 13. In Birdsnest," said Obie.

"Or, maybe the Owl in Accomack," offered Cindy.

"How about you?"

"I'm going back to Richmond Friday night. I've got laundry and need to check my mail."

Obie went running early Friday afternoon to be done before the cafeteria closed. He enjoyed the Friday menus, because it was seafood day. Fried shrimp, corn, and string beans preceded the blueberry, layered gelatin salad. Al Fowler had completed his rotation and packed up for Norfolk. Cindy and Bob had both left for Richmond. Obie had the apartment to himself. He talked to Priscilla on the phone while halfway watching the Winter

Olympics. He missed her immensely and they talked for nearly thirty minutes. She was going to leave early Saturday so they could meet for lunch.

After rounding Saturday morning, Obie drove to the Candlelight Inn and booked a twenty-one-dollar room for the night. This was not tourist season, and the motel was practically deserted. He considered shacking up in the student-dorm apartment, but, with his luck, a new Eastern Virginia student would show up or Cindy or Bob would return and it would look sleazy, especially in a community hospital that disallowed beer.

Obie hung out in the front lobby, walking back and forth from the doctor's lounge, where he would read over an EKG, then check back at the lobby. Priscilla finally arrived, beige nylon coat and jeans on. He embraced her in the front entrance and rode out with her to park. Somehow, having been close to people dying the past week, Obie seemed starved for "life". He longed to be close to, to touch, and to feel the warmth of another person. His desire for Priscilla was even more intense than that resulting from the physical, two-week separation. After relaxing together briefly in the students' quarters, Obie took Priscilla for a ride. He wanted to see the Chesapeake Bay, curious as to the effect of the past two weeks of subfreezing weather.

They found their way to the bay at Silver Beach and a panoramic arctic landscape greeted them. The shoreline was frozen with rough, white, chunky ice covering the salt water out two hundred to three hundred feet from the beach. The sun was bright, but the air still crisp and frigid. The water of the bay was deep blue below a vivid sky. Priscilla stood along the shore as Obie stepped slowly out onto the ice. His footing was awkward due to the irregular, jagged surface. About fifty feet out from the beach, he stopped, suddenly wondering how deep the water was under his feet.

Frozen Chesapeake Bay at Silver Beach, 1980

The Winter Olympic Games were showing on the projection TV at Nelson's Pizza. The US was hosting in Lake Placid.

"The spaghetti's not bad, but it's not Bella Italia," Priscilla reported, comparing it to her favorite Richmond restaurant.

"Nope. But it's not bad for the North Pole."

The Candlelight Inn was not well insulated, and a bitter draft flowed around the window-mounted AC unit conveniently overhanging the bed. It was, apparently, equipped to cater to the summer tourists. The heater ran continuously, with the fan blades knocking loudly against the sides. It produced, at best, tepid air. They moved quickly from the shower to the bed, sliding into the cool sheets and pulling the double covers up to their necks. Priscilla had donned her winter sleep attire, the full-length flannel gown with thick, wool socks. Obie wore his standard, cotton boxer shorts, hoping to enjoy some body-friction heat. Even the adverse weather could not keep them from fulfilling their lust, fueled by the two-week separation. A single encounter, however, was enough.

Sunday morning found the Eastern Shore dusted with powdery snow that had sneaked in during the cold night. Indeed, it was like dust as the dry air blew sprays of white crystals across the highway. Obie and Priscilla sat in the NAM Hospital cafeteria sipping after-breakfast coffee, enjoying each other's company. They found Cindy in the students' quarters, having driven back late Saturday. She had heard the forecast and feared driving across a twenty-three mile, snow-covered bridge over the waters of the Chesapeake Bay. They talked with Priscilla about their physician preceptors and the hospital.

Priscilla enjoyed hearing the M-81s discussing the physicians as if they were associates or colleagues. Medical students were the lowest level of clinicians at MCV, with interns, residents, attendings, and specialists all filling higher ranks. Here, at a rural community hospital, med students were more highly regarded as members of the health-care team. Priscilla could see a glimmer of the future and began to envision Obie as a budding doctor. He actually appeared to be changing these past two weeks.

The three of them returned to the frozen shore at Silver Beach, Obie equipped with his Minolta 35 mm camera. The small amount of snow had rendered the ice formation even more spectacular, contrasting against the now blue gray water and sky hosting mounds of white and gray clouds. Cindy was awed by the sight. The view was so glorious that, for a few minutes, they were oblivious to the twenty-six-degree temperature and the wind. Obie imagined that the frozen arctic would look like this, only year round.

Obie longed to have more time with Priscilla, but knew that she faced crossing the Bay Bridge Tunnel in these arctic weather conditions. He wanted her to complete that part of her drive in daylight. The roads were fairly clear, since the snow was less than an inch deep and had blown off the pavement, settling in ditches and drifts alongside the road. He bade her farewell at three thirty and insisted that she call him as soon as she was home.

"You can always stay another night at the Candlelight Inn," he offered.

"No, thanks! The heater in my car is warmer than that shack. I'll be okay. Besides, I've got to check on Motley." Motley was her cat.

Obie was enjoying a beer after his chilling run when Bob returned at dusk. Bob brought most of another six pack with him and joined Obie with a beer. Cindy came out and dropped a catalog on the coffee table in front of them.

"You guys can look over this if you want. I was just going to trash it. Thought you might enjoy browsing in Frederick's of Hollywood."

"You're not going to order anything?" asked Obie.

"Nope. They're made for taller girls with long legs. Their stuff doesn't fit me."

Obie thought Cindy was cute, even a little sexy. She was, however, only about five feet tall. The Frederick's models looked like they had four feet of legs alone, accentuated by four- to six-inch high heels.

"So a fashion show would be out of the question," probed Bob.

Cindy smiled and turned back toward her room. As she walked off, she looked back over her shoulder and swished her hips side to side, as if on the fashion runway.

In place of the Wednesday-afternoon lecture, Dr. Stith sent Obie to Dr. Gordon's pediatrics office. Dr. Gordon welcomed Obie and said, "Did you bring a coat and a camera?"

"No, why?" he asked.

"We're going to fly over to Tangier Island for the clinic. Get your stuff and be back here in ten minutes."

Dr. Gordon was small to medium build, with brown hair and a mustache. He told Obie about the island during the brief drive to the airfield, about three miles from the hospital.

"It's a small island of about nine hundred people, mostly watermen. There's a clinic there, but no doctor. A medical doctor from White Stone flies over on Thursdays to see patients—Dr. Nichols. I try to go on Wednesday afternoons, once or twice a month."

Dr. Gordon flew a single-engine Cessna Cub the twenty-minute flight over the Chesapeake Bay. The rough, ice-crusted shore looked smooth from eight thousand feet, and it sparkled in the sun. The island had a long strip of narrow, sandbar-like beach projecting south that was as long as the remainder of the island. After landing on the deserted airstrip, they walked the half-mile to the clinic, with Obie feeling useful carrying Dr. Gordon's suitcase-sized medical bag. The clinic was small and chilled, not wasting heat on a building that was usually vacant. Obie looked about at the brown paneling and near-antique equipment. Dr. Gordon lit the oil stove and cut on the lights.

"Do you have appointments?" asked Obie.

"Naw. I just see whoever shows up."

"Well, how do they know you're here?"

"An airplane lands on an island that's three miles long—everybody knows."

"Oh … Yeah."

"Listen, Obie. I don't know if you'll ever visit here again. I won't be very busy here. Take off! Look around the area. I'll see you back here in an hour or two."

Obie walked around and took pictures of the church, some of the docks, and the wooden, cage-like structures. These crab pots were used to hold crabs until they molted their hard shells and became vulnerable, soft-shelled crabs. They were then harvested before their shells hardened. The winter weather had rendered the streets deserted—a bicycle lay on the shoulder near a house.

When he returned to the clinic, it was almost warm inside.

"Did you have many patients?" asked Obie.

"Only four. The cold weather probably keeps some at home."

"Not worth the trip, hardly."

"Well, it's kinda fun. The people are so appreciative, and it makes my plane a tax write-off."

Back on the shore, the Eastern Virginia Medical School students were on spring break, and Bob was out for drinks at

Nelson's Pizza. Obie sat with a Michelob Light, thumbing through the Fredrick's catalogue. He looked up as Cindy walked out from her bedroom. She wore a large, black-and-gray football jersey that extended to just above her knees. Obie noticed the way the fabric fell across her chest and the jiggle as she walked, signaling that her breasts were bare under the jersey. Taking a beer from the refrigerator, she sat on the sofa bedside Obie. He was thrilled that she was comfortable enough with his company to walk around braless and help herself to the beer. He wondered, as she sat there, if she had on shorts, panties, or nothing under the long tail of the jersey.

"So, are you engaged to Priscilla?" she asked.

"Well, not officially. I guess 'pre-engaged' would be right. She has my college fraternity pin."

"Oh." She paused, staring off ahead. "The good guys are always taken."

Obie looked at Cindy, and she slowly turned and met his gaze. They both smiled, and Obie put his arm around her shoulders. They leaned back against the couch. He thought, fleetingly, who would ever know if they slept together? One hundred and forty miles from Richmond, on this isolated, rural peninsula? … He would know.

Obie left Nassawadox rejuvenated, enriched by the unique mix of medicine, rural living, the natural beauty of the Eastern Shore, and deeper friendships with his classmates. The third year was now over half-completed. He was certain that country people were the ones he wanted to practice among. Obie was anxious to see Priscilla, especially after holding at bay his growing desire for Cindy. He felt good. He drove straight to Priscilla's apartment at Dunston Manor.

Priscilla hugged him as he entered, but her smile quickly dissolved. She resembled a zombie, looking up at him with blank, water-filled eyes.

"Kathy Newman is dead," she said. "Overdosed yesterday."

Dooley Hospital, MCV, 1979

Chapter 10
Pediatrics and St. Mary's

Kathy Newman's memorial service was in the college chapel, Monumental Church, on Wednesday afternoon. Appropriately, Monumental Church was built as a memorial to seventy-two people who died on the site in a theater fire. This was a solemn gathering of medical students and MCV staff. There were probably one hundred mourners gathered as the VCU chaplain led the service. The studs looked at one another in the surreal atmosphere, so different from the classrooms and wards where they usually met. Dark suits and dresses replaced the white jackets. Having learned so many medical secrets instilled a feeling of immortality and invincibility in them. This tragedy dealt a heavy blow, awakening the M-81s with the cold reality that they, too, are vulnerable—even at increased risk of dying due to the level of stress and long hours they endured. Obie felt a grim void inside … an emptiness … so much so that, when his gaze met John's, he was speechless. They each shook their head slowly.

Outside of the memorial service, there was no break in the clinical rotations. Having completed orientation that Monday, Obie had begun work in the pediatrics ER. The patient-care area reminded him of an old school with its hallway and classroom-like treatment rooms. The ceilings were eleven feet high, and bulletin boards adorned the corridor walls. The colors were earth tones, and the treatment rooms had wood-paneled doors with large, single-paned, frosted-glass windows.

Jim Beam and John Morgan were the fellow M-81s rotating in the peds ER. Dr. Rachel Cooper was the pediatrics resident, AR, in charge of the peds ER. Obie thought a female would be a natural for a pediatrician, given that they possess certain maternal instincts and a nurturing nature.

"I want you each to see a couple of patients with me first to get a feel for treating kids. Then you can do initial evaluations. The patients can't usually give you any history, so the parents or guardians are a key part in the workup," began Dr. Cooper. She was medium build with shoulder-length, straw-colored hair and black-rimmed, reading-type glasses riding low on her nose. She had a distinct business air about her. She motioned to Jim Beam, and they disappeared into exam room two.

Obie and John stood in the nurses' area as an eight-year-old male was led into another exam room by a nurse. He was making wheezing sounds as he breathed, pausing at the scales for the nurse to record his weight.

John leaned toward Obie. "March, and the spring asthma season is in bloom," he said.

"Oh."

"She got his weight to calculate his epinephrine dose," continued John.

Sure enough, as Dr. Cooper emerged from exam room two, the nurse addressed her.

"Wheezing in room three. Seventy-two pounds."

Dr. Cooper quickly stepped into room three, listened to the child's chest, and called out, "Get 0.3 cc epinephrine, nasal

O$_2$, and some juice!" She turned to the studs and said, "Asthma protocol is: epinephrine 0.01 cc per kilogram, up to three doses, fifteen minutes apart until lungs are clear. If this doesn't clear them: aminophylline IV over thirty minutes, then recheck in one hour. If they're still wheezing, admit them."

"What about steroids?" asked John.

"If they get admitted, they get an aminophylline drip, IV hydration, and steroids. Steroids don't work fast enough for the ER."

It was very educational for Obie to work with Dr. Cooper and learn how to obtain medical histories on children by questioning parents. Physicians are scientists and need data, numbers, specific symptoms, when symptoms began, and how many episodes of vomiting or diarrhea have occurred. Pediatric medical histories invariably begin with, "Oh, he's been real sick for a while now." Rachel Cooper was seasoned enough to cultivate the main ailment and weed out the insignificant items offered by the guardians. Sorting through the guardian's story to home in on a diagnosis depended on the specifics in the medical history, as well as the physical findings.

"You have to have a rectal reading to know a baby's temperature. Oral and underarm, axillary, readings are just not accurate enough. Too many variables will affect the reading: drinking liquids, mouth-breathing, sweating," said Dr. Cooper. She added with a raised brow, "Grandmothers, however, are quite good at sensing a temperature. Usually within one degree." This was more evidence to Obie's maternal instinct belief.

After a day of shadowing Dr. Cooper, the students began doing initial assessments. Obie was a little hesitant to begin pediatric evaluations alone, but felt the need to test the waters. He was now familiar with the asthma-treatment protocol and counting out the vomiting and diarrhea episodes to assess for dehydration. He picked up the clipboard for Matthew Clayton, age four, with the complaint of "flu symptoms," took a deep breath, and entered exam room six.

"Hi. I'm Student Doctor Hardy. Is this Matthew Clayton?"

"Yes," answered Matthew's mother. She was a slender white woman with straight black hair to her shoulder. She appeared disheveled, with dusky circles under her eyes. The "student doctor" title had not impressed her. "This is Matt," she stated.

The young child she had identified was lying on the exam table, a wooden platform attached to the room's corner, two sides bordered by walls. He looked quite ill, and a smell of stale vomit lingered in the air. His sandy hair was awry, his skin pale, and his lips dry.

"He started with a cold about ten days ago," began his mother.

Obie quickly noted that "a cold" was not a specific enough symptom and probed, "What type of cold symptoms did he have?"

"Well … just a runny nose and some cough."

"Any earache, sore throat, or fever?"

"No. Well, maybe he was a little warm. I gave him some baby aspirin. He seemed a little better until yesterday. He's been vomiting and groggy. Sleeping. And today he is confused. He kicked at me and says things like, 'The birds are too flappy.'"

Obie managed to get a look in the ear that was positioned upward, but, when trying to get Matt to roll over, the little boy began twisting about, pushing away, and groaning. The examination was limited at best. Obie was puzzled as to the diagnosis. His nervous system symptoms resembled meningitis, but he had no fever. The other symptoms seemed like an intestinal virus, like the stomach flu. He presented his findings to Dr. Cooper.

"Any recent illness before he began vomiting?" she asked.

"Well, yeah. His mom reported an upper respiratory infection eight or nine days before."

"Did he get any treatment for it?"

"No. Just some aspirin. I think."

"Aspirin?" she retorted. "Let's see him now!" She led the way back to room six. With Obie and Matt's mother assisting, she did a more thorough exam and then addressed his mother. "We need to do some tests on Matt—blood tests and a spinal tap. That's testing the fluid from around the spinal cord for signs of infection. He will probably have to be admitted."

His mother nodded understandingly. After exiting the room, Dr. Copper spoke to Obie, "I doubt that it's meningitis, but we can't rule it out without the tap. We'll get a blood culture, CBC, chemistries, and an ammonia level." Obie recalled doing ammonia levels on advanced liver-disease patients on the medical wards. He looked quizzical.

"Ammonia level?"

"Yeah. He could have Reye's Syndrome."

Their workup showed normal, clear spinal fluid, normal white blood cell count, and mildly elevated liver enzymes. The ammonia level would not be back until twenty-four hours. All findings indicated Reye's Syndrome.

"How do you treat Reye's Syndrome?" asked Obie.

"Mostly supportive care," said Cooper. "He's in stage two—confusion and delirium. Stages four and five carry a 50 percent mortality rate."

John Morgan, listening with fascination, asked, "Do steroids help any?"

"No," continued Cooper. "There's no evidence of it helping. We do use mannitol for brain swelling in stages three and higher."

Later, John spoke to Obie about his son. "Derrick's had a respiratory virus. I told my wife not to give him any aspirin."

"Yeah. Good thing," said Obie. "How old is Derrick?"

"Two and a half. He was a diaphragm-failure baby. We named him Derrick because *diaphragm* starts with a *D*, so we'll remember. Oh, I need to remember to take my otoscope home and check his ears. I leave it in my locker here."

On the way to the student parking lot, Obie stopped by the MCV post office on Ninth and Marshall. He shuffled through his mail, noting his bank statement, community medicine grade (a pass), and another envelope printed with a MCV letterhead. It was from the blood bank department. His summer research preceptor in 1978 was the head of the MCV Blood Bank, Dr. Ali Hossaini. Their project involved testing plant substances for toxic effects on different types of cells. The "selective cytotoxicity of plant lectins" is how Dr. Hossaini phrased it. Obie had continued the study on Wednesday afternoons his second year of school. Dr. Hossaini had given him free run of the lab during this time.

The letter invited Obie to write up an abstract, or summary report, of their findings to submit to the Virginia Society of Hematology. Obie was excited about an opportunity to contribute to medical science and validate his hours of dabbling in the lab. He drove straight to Priscilla's apartment to tell her.

"Wow!" she said. "What will happen if you submit this research paper?"

"He says that, if it's accepted, we might go to Virginia Beach and present it at their annual meeting."

"You know, you used some of my blood in those tests too," she reminded him. He had, indeed, used Priscilla's, Dr. Hossaini's, and his own blood as normal controls for comparison with leukemia patients.

"And I thank you again for your contribution. I'll mention your name at my Nobel Prize acceptance."

The next morning, Dr. Cooper updated them on Matt. During the night he had become comatose and had a seizure. John had been on call and placed a nasogastric tube down into the stomach. Through it, they had started giving him lactulose treatments in an effort to lower the ammonia production in the bowels. He appeared to be stable now, with no more seizures, but was not very responsive. His mother stayed at his bedside in the pediatric ICU continuously. She stroked his head and held his hand. Obie realized that Matt's mortality risk was now quite high. He wondered why MCV, the "Miracle College," couldn't do more for Matt.

At lunchtime, Obie went by Dr. Hossaini's office to accept his proposal and start planning. Hossaini was short, a little stocky, and wore wire-rimmed glasses. He always had a wide smile and was nearly beaming when Obie arrived. He was of Middle Eastern heritage, but only a trace of an accent remained.

"Obie, I'm glad to see you again."

"Well, I miss your lab on Wednesday afternoons."

"So, are you interested?"

"Sure! It'd be great to show off what we've done."

"Well, I knew you'd need time for the literature search and all. The audiovisual lab will make up any slides or graphs we need if we get to do the presentation."

"Thanks for this opportunity. I really enjoyed playing scientist in the lab, and I'd like to see something come of it."

"Very well. Check with me each week, 'cause we'll need the abstract written by May 8."

Obie was on call that night and kept checks on Matt Clayton. By suppertime, Matt was alert, and the NG tube was pulled out. He drank some juice and ate a popsicle. By morning rounds, he was walking around in his room and was moved from the pediatric ICU, "Pick-U," to the general pediatrics floor.

"Kids get well so fast!" Obie said to John.

"Yeah. They get sick fast too," John added.

"How's Derrick?"

"Well, Sam chewed me out. I forgot the otoscope again, and his eardrum burst from an infection."

"Oh, no. I can't believe that!"

"Well, they say, 'The shoemaker's kids go barefoot.' Too busy seeing other folks' kids to see after my own." John looked serious and sad. Obie realized that John, as a M-81, couldn't have prescribed any treatment.

"You couldn't have given him an antibiotic, anyway," consoled Obie.

"But I could've got him seen *sooner* if I knew he had otitis media."

"Well, would that have prevented his perforation?"

"I don't know," he answered, but he did know it would have prevented some of the guilt he now carried.

In the peds ER, Jim Beam began working up a sickle-cell-crisis patient, the first admission of his on-call day. John went into room three, a child named Wesley Dokes, a two-year-old with "fever" listed on his clipboard. He discovered Wesley had cerebral palsy and a seizure disorder and could only speak a few words. John did a careful exam and, most certainly, included the ear exam. He pulled back on the ear cartilage to straighten out the ear canal and peek through the otoscope window. The eardrum did not align easily, and he maneuvered the scope and ear cartilage around, trying to fully visualize the eardrum. He was damn sure he would not miss another otitis media infection. Wesley was a little fidgety initially but had settled down. In fact, he didn't seem to be moving at all. After a good look at a normal-appearing eardrum, John removed the scope and was preparing to check the opposite ear. Wesley was motionless, limp, and dusky colored. His mother grabbed him suddenly and shook his shoulders.

"Wesley! Wesley! Breathe!" she cried out. Wesley began trembling and moaning, his eyes rolling to the left side. John opened the door and called out.

"Dr. Cooper! Emergency in room three! Seizure!"

Dr. Cooper rushed in as the trembling was subsiding and Mrs. Dokes was giving some mouth-to-mouth breaths. John was frozen—shocked by the scenario.

"I was checking his ears when … "

"Checking his ears?" cut in Dr. Cooper. "This is Wesley Dokes! He always stops breathing if you look in his ears!" Dr. Cooper felt for a femoral pulse as Mrs. Dokes paused in her rescue breathing. "He'll be okay now. Thanks, Mrs. Dokes." Wesley was breathing, and life's color refilled his body. Racheal Cooper turned to John as they exited the room, "If he comes in with an upper respiratory infection and a fever, we just treat him for possible otitis. It's safer than the risk of precipitating a seizure with an ear exam. He has an exaggerated autonomic vagal reflex that stops his breathing."

Saturday rounds introduced a weekend attending, a staff pediatrician who had a private practice in the west end. Dr. Terry Lovelette was a mildly overweight man in his late thirties. He wore a nylon knit gray shirt with an unbuttoned collar, no tie, and a gold-banded watch and three gold rings. After two abbreviated, "weekend-format" admission presentations, Dr. Lovelette led the group on rounds. They did doorway reviews of the other patients. Matt Clayton was cleared for discharge after running impishly out of his room through the encircled team at his doorway. As they completed their circuit, Dr. Lovelette looked at his gold watch.

"Well, 9:35. Not bad for Saturday." Then, looking up, he said, "Okay, which student was on last night?"

"Me," answered Jim Beam.

"Okay, go home. You're done. Who's on tonight?"

"I am," answered John.

"Okay, you help with ward scut and the new workups today; and you," he looked at Obie's name tag, "Hardy? Let's go get some coffee."

"All right."

Obie followed Dr. Lovelette across the Eleventh and Marshall intersection to the Skull and Bones Restaurant. They sat at a booth and each had coffee and a danish. Dr. Lovelette began his dissertation.

"I'm going to tell you all you need to know to be a good pediatrician or family physician." He talked about otitis media, ear infections, and the appropriate antibiotic choices. Unresponsive cases after the third antibiotic and cases after a third recurrence get referred to ENT, or ear, nose, and throat. The asthma regimen of three adrenalin shots, aminophylline, and then steroids was reviewed. Stomach viruses and gastroenteritis are slowly hydrated following a two-hour gut rest after puking. Use clear liquids—no dairy products, citrus, or soups. After twelve hours, restart the

BRAPT diet, things beginning with *B-R-A-P-T* letters, like bread, rice, applesauce, potatoes, peaches, and toast. He even included a plan for adolescent acne. "The immunization schedules, growth charts, developmental milestones are all in the textbooks. What I've talked about will let you treat 90 percent of your pediatric problems."

These guidelines made sense and were the most practical items Obie had heard on this rotation. He thanked Dr. Lovelett, emphasizing his appreciation of this lesson.

"Sure. We need doctors who can do good general care. Now, are you married?"

Obie had noted the gold jewelry and neat attire of Terry Lovelett, as well as his genderless first name. He didn't want to make rash assumptions.

"No, sir. I've got a girlfriend, though."

"Good. Nurture your relationship! Good doctors don't take enough personal time; they're too dedicated to medicine. Show her how much you care about her."

"Okay. I'll try to give her more attention. But you know our call schedule here."

"Sure. All the more reason. Well, it's been nice talking with you. Good luck with pediatrics."

"Thanks. And thanks for everything."

Obie had learned more practical pediatrics in the hour of coffee chat than over the past two weeks of his pediatrics rotation. Now he had some free time to begin the literature search for his research paper. He grabbed his knapsack and walked up Twelfth Street to the Tompkins McCaw Library.

Tompkins McCaw Library, MCV Campus

The 1932 building was a modernized reference library with Xerox copying machines and microfilm viewers. Obie began his arduous task with the Index Medicus, an index of all published articles listed by subject and key words. He needed to look back several years to best assure a comprehensive search. From his list of articles, he would individually find the abstracts, or summaries, and review them to determine which articles were actually pertinent to his project. The library closed at six on Saturdays but was open later on Sundays and weekdays.

Obie found only fifteen articles of significant relevancy and went to the front desk for assistance. Tompkins McCaw stocked nine of the abstracts he sought, and would have to order the others.

"How much are the ordered copies?" Obie asked.

"Two dollars each, and we can have them in three business days."

"Okay," said Obie. "I'll come by Monday with the order and money."

"Do you want the originals?" asked the clerk. "Or the English translations?"

Obie had noticed that two of the articles' titles looked German or Swedish. "Ah,… the English," he answered.

"English translations may take seven to ten business days."

He was then directed to the "stacks" rooms to sort through the abstracts, bound by journal name and year.

"The abstracts can't be checked out, but you can make copies here for ten cents each."

Obie noted the coin operated copiers and felt in his pocket. Two dimes. "Can I get change for a dollar?" he asked the clerk.

"No. We don't make change for the copiers."

He had planned to call Priscilla from the payphone at the library entrance. It cost a dime. Two abstracts or one abstract and a call? Dr. Lovelett's advice on relationships faded. He needed to get as much data as possible, so he headed for the stacks.

"So, you spent the afternoon at the library?" asked Priscilla that evening over supper. "When you could've been with me?"

"Well, I've got to get this literature search done before I can write the paper."

"And you're on call tomorrow?"

"Well, yeah. I'm sorry, Priscilla. We're here now. Let's not fuss. The paper will be done in six weeks. The second half of my peds I'll be at Saint Mary's, five or six miles from the medical library."

She understood how important the chance to publish a research paper was to Obie. Medical school, however, was always a major intrusion in their relationship. This was yet another imposition.

"Only six weeks, huh? I guess we'll see."

Saint Mary's Hospital was a pleasant commute down Monument Avenue. The dogwoods were in bloom, the air warming, and the patio dining area off of the cafeteria was inviting. The medical students ate most lunches on the patio, when seating allowed. Jim Beam joined Obie, as well as Micheal Rhone. Michael was tall, about six foot two and somewhat stout, with dark hair and a mustache. Their pediatric JAR was Randy Preston, of medium build, with black hair beginning to recede. He had a square jaw and was wearing a light blue dress shirt with no tie.

"Saint Mary's is a lot different from MCV," started Dr. Preston in the conference room. "We do the scut work for the private pediatricians. I often have to call them to approve the orders, and they make the medical decisions when they round. Critical cases usually get transferred to the MCV PICU."

The studs were asked to pick up some patients on the floor to follow until they had new admissions. Obie reviewed the chart of Jason Youngblood, a twelve-month-old with pneumonia. He went in to introduce himself and found Jason playing with toys in his crib bed, with IV secured to his left forearm. His mother was standing beside the bed, smiling. She was a beautiful girl in her early twenties, with caramel-colored hair cascading in curls onto her shoulders. Her white-and-orange-flowered sundress showed the smooth skin of her neck and upper torso. Obie forced his gaze to meet her eyes, trying to avoid staring at her bosom cleavage. Her wholesome complexion was accented by perfectly applied, glossy lipstick and lightly lined eyelids framing hazel eyes. Jason had no more fever and was eating now. It appeared he might go home in a day or two. Obie returned to the conference to complete his patient index card notes and sighed as he sat down.

"What's up?" asked Randy Preston.

"Oh, nothing. I just saw Jason in room 321."

"Oh," said Randy, knowingly. "You met his mother."

"Oh, yeah!"

"Jason has 'GLM Syndrome'. It sometimes makes if hard to treat a child."

"'GLM Syndrome'? What's that?"

"Good-Looking Mom Syndrome," smiled Randy. Then, addressing the students, he asked, "Okay, who's on call tonight?"

"I am," answered Michael Rhone.

"Okay, come with me. They're starting a C-section downstairs."

Rhone was not only tall, he carried an air of confidence—of seasoned training. He appeared to be more a doctor than just an M-81, third-year student. Randy Preston reviewed their protocols for newborn care as they scrubbed in. They just put scrubs over top of their street clothes, since they would only be needed fifteen or twenty minutes. The sky blue scrubs were a change from the surgical green and blue gray colors at MCV.

They stood by the receiving bassinette area and Dr. Preston checked the oxygen line, suction, and laryngoscope to assure readiness. The obstetrician was working behind him, exposing the uterus.

"Thick meconium fluid!" announced the obstetrician as the brownish-stained amniotic fluid gushed up from the incision. He pushed down on the abdomen to help maneuver the head through the opening. As soon as the head popped up, he suctioned out the mouth and nose before completing the delivery. The scrub nurse quickly deposited the newborn onto the bassinette table and called out.

"Eleven forty-two delivery."

Randy positioned the infant's head and put in the laryngoscope to visualize the trachea.

"Meconium in trachea," he announced. Michael handed him the size three ET tube, which he inserted.

"I've got the Delee suction," said Michael, reaching out for the ET tube. He attached the Delee to the ET tube and sucked on the other end with his mouth. A few greenish particles appeared in the clear plastic trap in the Delee, and Michael pulled out the ET tube and suction tube together. Randy looked again with the laryngoscope.

"Trachea clear now," he reported. "Good job," he said to Michael.

The infant gasped twice and began crying, his dusky color beginning to pinken and limbs flexing up as muscle tone increased.

Michael felt the left arm for a pulse.

"Heart rate 110," he announced. "One-minute Apgar … seven, maybe?"

"'Seven' sounds good," replied Randy. "One off each for color, tone, and respiratory effort."

Later, on their way back from the nursery, Dr. Preston spoke to Michael. "That was a good job in the delivery room, Rhone."

"Well, we've done OB already. I've helped on three C-sections. Also, my daughter was born two months ago by forceps delivery. My wife had induced labor for premature rupture of membranes and went into fetal distress."

"Oh, man! I'm sorry."

"Both mother and daughter have done well."

"Good. I'm glad."

Obie had Saturday night call duty. The afternoon was fairly quiet after rounds, and he read up on pediatric rashes, the three *R*s—Rubeola (measles), Rubella (German measles), Roseola—and others. There was a television in the corner of the conference room with a video-cassette player—to review educational tapes, no doubt. The TV was receiving broadcast programs that day, like the running of the Kentucky Derby. The announcers speculated as to what chances the day's winner, Genuine Risk, had to win the next two races to capture the triple crown. Fans had been spoiled by two triple crown winners in the seventies—Secretariat and Seattle Slew. It could be a decade before the feat was repeated.

Rachel Cooper, the covering JAR for the weekend, stepped into the room.

"We've got a couple of kids down in the ER. Come on."

"Okay," answered Obie, following her down the hall.

"The first one's asthma. She's kinda tight," she said as they walked into the ER. "She's over in bed four. Amy Queen. Check on her while I see the fever and rash."

"Okay," answered Obie. He found her chart and looked it over. She hadn't received but one epinephrine and no IV aminophylline. He talked to Amy, a six-year-old girl, and her mother. When he listened to Amy's lungs, there was no wheezing. This wasn't the MCV protocol of three epinephrines, aminophylline, and admit if not clear. He was going to find Dr. Cooper when a man with sandy hair and a neatly trimmed mustache approached him.

"You got Amy Queen's chart?" he asked.

"Yes, sir. Obie Hardy, third-year student," he greeted.

"Gary Peters. I'm Amy's pediatrician."

"Oh. Great." Obie, hesitantly, presented his dilemma. "She's had just one epi, and she's not wheezing. What do you think about some Susphrine and Alupent?"

Dr. Peters smiled slyly and invited Obie back to the bedside. "She breathes shallow and slow, so you can't hear the wheezes. She doesn't want to be admitted. Here, listen." He placed Obie's stethoscope on Amy's back and asked her to take a deep breath. When she began to exhale, he squeezed her chest, pushing front to back. Obie heard the wheezes.

He followed Dr. Peters back to the desk and watched as he wrote orders.

"It's called the 'forced expiratory wheeze,'" said Peters. "It's useful when they're moving too little air to wheeze … or if they're trying to fool you."

"Thanks," answered Obie.

Dr. Cooper came up and greeted Dr. Peters as he was leaving. She then turned to Obie and said, "The other child has a fever and a rash. I'm not sure what it is yet."

Obie went to evaluate Cory Windsor, a five-year-old boy sitting with his mother. Obie had just been reading about rashes and studying the photos in Nelson's textbook, the green book. He was eager to apply his learning. Cory's rash, however, was not the textbook type. Obie's enthusiasm waned. Cory looked sickly with red, tearing eyes and lips that looked badly chapped. There were large lymph glands in his neck and groin area. The rash was pink and splotchy, scattered over his torso and extremities. He had a temperature of 101, having run a fever for five days now.

Obie returned to the charting area of the ER with a puzzled look. Dr. Cooper smiled wisely and said, "Well, what have we got here?"

"I don't know. Measles usually has a cough. Rubella can swell the neck glands, but not the eyes and lips. Fifth's Disease usually has the red, slapped-cheeks look. He doesn't fit any of the pictures."

"Okay. He has inflamed lips and conjunctivae, the mucous membranes. Also, the skin rash and enlarged lymph nodes. Ever heard of 'Muco-Cutaneous Lymph Node Syndrome'?"

"I'm not sure. Sounds weird."

"Otherwise called 'Kawasaki's Disease'?" Obie was surprised when he saw her order aspirin twice a day for Cory.

"What about aspirin causing Reye's Syndrome?" he asked.

"Well, Reye's is more closely linked to influenza B and coxsaki viruses. It could still be a risk, but Kawasaki's causes inflammation of the coronary arteries that can cause heart attacks."

"Heart attack? In a five-year-old?"

"Yep."

Obie sat at Priscilla's kitchen table, reviewing the notes from his abstracts and forming the reference list for his paper. Priscilla was on the kitchen phone.

"Sure, Daddy. I'll be there, I promise. It's great that you're gonna do it … Yes … I love you. Good night." She sat down across from Obie, smiling. "Daddy's been asked to dress out for D-day celebration on the battleship in Wilmington. He wants us to come."

"That's great!" answered Obie. "When is it?'

"The weekend of June 6."

"June sixth?" Obie suddenly began shuffling through some papers. He stopped, reading from a letter. "That's the same weekend my research presentation in Virginia Beach would be."

"Aw …" Priscilla moaned, her disappointment blatant.

"Well," Obie responded. "They haven't even reviewed my paper yet, much less accepted it for presentation."

Priscilla feared the six-week work period for this paper had already begun a menacing expansion.

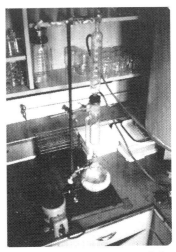

Soxolate extractor for making amygdalin (Laetrile)
from apricot pits

Chapter 11
Surgery and Research

The M-3 surgery rotation matched medicine in length, spanning twelve weeks, the longest clinical rotations of the year. Obie started his first month on general surgery, accompanied by Walter Ferguson. They rounded on West 3 and West 4, went to clinics in A. D. Williams, and scrubbed in on some cases. Dr. Harvey Sugarman was refining surgical treatment of obesity and placing his post-op patients on West 3. He had tried gastric balloons to fill the stomach, creating the sensation of fullness, but with little success. His gastric stapling was the newest procedure, making the stomach passageway very narrow, limiting the amount it could hold in a period of time. This made the stomach more of a conduit than a reservoir. West 3 was where these M-81s learned post-op care.

The risk factors for clots in the veins, thrombophlebitis,

included female sex, obesity, hormone therapy such as birth control pills, and smoking. Since this was the obesity ward, no one had fewer than two of these risk factors, and very few had uneventful recoveries. Popping open of the incision, wound dehiscence, afforded opportunities for M-81s to learn debridement, irrigation, and packing.

Dr. Richard Springer was the surgical JAR leading morning rounds. Surgical rounds began at six a.m. to allow the surgeons to be finished before the eight a.m. operating room start time.

"Ms. McLean is two-days status-post panniculectomy and has wound dehisence now," informed Dr. Springer. Obie wondered about the long incision across her abdomen, just below the waist line.

"Panniculectomy?" Obie whispered to Ferguson.

"The panniculus. You know, the spare tire, the fatty apron of the stomach," he answered. Obie grimaced with acknowledgement.

"You studs will power-spray the wound with half-strength peroxide daily. Then gauze-pack with saline moistened, wet-to-dry packing." This sounded simple, except that the incision was forty centimeters (16 inches) long, six centimeters (2 1/2 inches) deep, and was oozing a brownish gray substance. Thus, incision-wound dehiscence care for all the West-3 patients became the daily routine for the M-81s.

The surgical ER was the "Red ER." Obie remembered this easily by the association of red, blood, and surgery. On his first call night, he was sent to the Blue—the medical—ER. There was a patient with possible appendicitis for a surgical consult. Obie recognized Crystal Meriwether, the medical intern from his West-15 rotation. She had Blue ER duty for the night.

"Hardy," she greeted, "What brings you here tonight?"

"Surgical rotation. We're here for a consult," motioning toward Dr. Springer.

"Oh. That would be bed seven, Mr. Kaywood. Probable appendicitis."

"Thanks," answered Dr. Springer. They entered the glass-walled hub of the Blue ER, the fishbowl, and Dr. Meriwether produced the clipboard for bed seven. Obie could see Mr. Kaywood from inside the fishbowl; and Springer, after glancing over the chart, looked out at him as well. Mr. Kaywood had a scraggly beard, long hair, and a weathered face.

"Looks like a redneck," Dr. Springer stated. "Is he from North Carolina?"

"I don't know," said Meriwether. "Why?"

"Oh, I have a theory that all rednecks have at one time lived in a trailer in North Carolina."

Obie and Crystal exchanged quizzical looks. Dr. Springer strutted off to bed seven, Obie on his heels. Springer asked a few key questions and pressed on Mr. Kaywood's abdomen, eliciting the flinch-and-grimace characteristic of appendicitis. He then posed a few additional questions.

"Sir, do you live in a mobile home?"

"Yes, sir," answered Kaywood. "In Amelia."

"Okay. Amelia, huh? Well, have you ever lived in North Carolina?"

"No, sir."

"Honey," interjected his wife. "You did work a year for that logging company in Benson, North Carolina."

"Oh, yeah! I almost forgot that."

"Okay, then," said Dr. Springer. "We're going to have to remove your appendix tonight." They returned to the fishbowl, where he said to Obie, "Write up his H&P and I'll go set up the OR." Then, turning to Meriwether, he noted, "Trailer. Benson, North Carolina."

"So, Hardy," she said as Dr. Springer walked off, "I see you've met the Dick."

"'Dick'? Is that for 'Richard' Springer?"

"No, not 'Dick'. *The* Dick!"

Obie got to scrub in and hold a retractor for "the Dick's" appendectomy. He even got to cut the sutures as Dr. Springer closed the skin. Springer's pager sounded during the closure;

another case in the Red ER. Removing gloves, gown, and mask, he called out, "Hardy."

"Yeah?"

"Write up an op note, then meet me in the Red ER. Estimated blood loss, 200 cc."

"Sure thing." Obie remembered the OB delivery notes and outlined an op note using the same format. With Mr. Kaywood in recovery, Obie took the stairs down to the basement level, Red ER.

Just inside the double swinging doors, a large black policeman was questioning another black man who was sitting on a stretcher. The man's left leg was bandaged with a bright red splotch in the center of the gauze.

"Well, who shot you, sir?" There was no response from the stretcher man, who was ignoring the policeman. "Okay, how did you get shot? What happened?"

"I don't know," answered the wounded man.

"All right. There's only three things people shoot someone over. Money, drugs, or women. Which was it?"

After a long pause, he answered softly, "Money."

Their patient was a twenty-eight-year- old white female who was in a head-on collision. Although belted in the front seat, she had findings of internal abdominal bleeding.

"This is a trauma case," explained Dr. Springer. "Everybody will want to scrub in on it." Dr. A. B. Haynes was the attending on call and appeared outside the OR as Dr. Springer was scrubbing. He was an older man in his early sixties, but he stood straight and tall. A surgical intern and another resident scrubbed in. Obie watched from the perimeter as the OR team worked on the patient.

They promptly suctioned a canister of blood from the abdomen upon entering. Obie stood on a step stool, straining to see the action.

"There's no bleeding from the spleen," announced Springer, somewhat disappointed. He had positioned himself on the patient's left side, anticipating a ruptured spleen.

"No blood from the liver either," stated Dr. Haynes. "The capsule is intact." They began picking through the other abdominal contents, continuing to suction fresh blood from the exposed field. "Ah! The greater omentum! There's a mesenteric branch spurting."

"Well, that's weird," responded Springer.

As Dr. Haynes clamped the torn vessel, he continued, "The lap belt. The shearing force stretches and tears the omental vessels. It's unusual to see such bleeding, though."

Obie was impressed that this vehicular-safety feature was responsible for a life-threatening injury. The surgery took on a more routine air after the bleeding was subdued. Still, it was four thirty a.m. when the patient reached the recovery room. It was still too early to prepare for six a.m. rounds but too late to get more than a nap. Obie opted for the nap, only to be awakened at 5:10.

"Mr. Kaywood has been unable to void since surgery. He's getting uncomfortable and needs a foley catheter," reported the nurse.

Foley catheter insertion, a cup of bean, rounds, wound care, and scut work ensued. A full day despite only thirty minutes rest. Obie welcomed the afternoon, planning to bike home before dark. He exited West Hospital on Twelfth Street and walked over to the bike rack beside George Ben Johnston Auditorium. He stopped abruptly. The rack was empty. Did he leave his bike somewhere else? The severed chain lock still lying on the pavement assured him that his bike had been here.

There was no way to go home, and Priscilla was out to dinner with a friend, expecting that he would just crash for the night. She did, however, live on the bus route, and he had a key to her apartment. Obie walked the three blocks to the Broad Street bus stop and caught the bus for Forest Hill. He leaned his head against his backpack and rested his weary eyes. When he opened them to check the bus's progress, the road was not the familiar route. Had he caught the wrong bus? He saw Forest Hill Avenue on a road sign, realizing he had been asleep and passed his stop by a mile or so. He decided to stay on board, hoping the bus would continue back to his stop. It did, after another twenty minutes.

Priscilla returned about nine o'clock to find Obie asleep on the steps in her apartment alcove.

"Obie? How'd you get here?"

"Huh?" he slurred, barely awakening. "My bike was stolen. I rode the bus here,… but I forgot my key is back at the COOP."

Sunday found Obie finishing his research paper, which had to be submitted by the next week. The fact that Dr. Hossaini had obtained some Laetrile from Mexico had bothered him. He discovered that anyone seriously mentioning Laetrile was black-balled from medical circles. It was viewed as charlatan, quackery, and an exploitation of desperate cancer patients. He was glad that the data he had presented at Kinloch Nelson Student Honors Day had not shown it effective. In fact, after the lukewarm reception of his presentation, he had resented Dr. Hossaini for associating him with Laetrile. The original study had only nine leukemic patients. He had raised the number to fifteen by continuing the project on Wednesday afternoons during his second year of med school. Now, collating the additional test samples, something was a bit different. One of the test solutions seemed to show increased cell lysis, or death, for leukemic cells. This solution, however, was not Laetrile, but an extract Obie had made from apricot pits in an effort to produce the controversial drug. Obie's apricot-pit dialysate was killing leukemic cells, and Laetrile was not.

"Yes! Yes! By all means!" exclaimed Dr. Hossaini when Obie asked about the additional data. "Include the new test results in the paper."

"Okay, but it's due Friday. I don't know if I have enough time."

"Just report the numbers. We won't need the charts or graphs until the presentation. We'll have another month to work them up."

Obie found that the apricot-pit dialysate, DIA, killed 97 percent of acute lymphocytic leukemia—ALL—cells and 70 percent of acute myelogenous leukemia—AML—cells. The probability value, or p value, shows the likelihood of the differences between two tested items being mere chance or coincidence. Scientific results are more significant the lower the p value, usually striving for 0.01 or less. Obie calculated the p value for ALL-cell lysis from DIA to be 0.044 and the AML-cell lysis, 0.134. Obie's results were certainly not Nobel Prize contenders but nonetheless showed the odds of the toxic effect being real were about 96 and 87 percent.

He typed up the one-page abstract and completed the four-page paper and the reference list on his old Remington typewriter. It looked official in the clear plastic binder, and, immediately after morning rounds, he dropped it off at Dr. Hossaini's office.

"Great job," said Dr. Hossaini, grinning. "Here, Obie," he added, holding out a newspaper article, "read this when you get a chance. I'll get this paper submitted today."

Obie stood in OR four beside John Morgan, looking at two incisions spanning the length of the inside of a left leg and thigh. John was showing Obie the running-lockstitch suture for closing a vein-donor site.

"Use the 4-0 nylon, taking big bites about a centimeter apart," he said. Obie copied this maneuver along the calf wound as John methodically inched along the thigh incision. Their progress was slowed a little by the intermittent, inquisitive peeks at the patient's open chest with slow, cold-stunned heartbeats. "You know what the most common surgery done at MCV is?" queried John.

"I dunno. Appendectomies?" he answered.

"Nope. These cases. Coronary bypasses. They use two ORs, equipped with the heart-lung bypass machines. Two four-hour cases in each daily; four cases a day."

Obie was a little awed. The coronary-artery bypass graph,

known as CABG, or "cabbage," was still in its infancy. Long-term studies on mortality and heart-attack prevention were still ongoing. Only patients with three-vessel disease were candidates for the procedure. Heart disease, nevertheless, was still the number-one killer in America.

John Morgan was rotating on the cardiovascular surgical service, and his experience was obvious. He was about three-fourths finished closing his incision while Obie was barely half done. When he finished, he began suturing on the far end of Obie's work point.

"I'll start at this end and meet you," he said. "We gotta hurry. They're putting the wires in the chest wall now."

Obie glanced up at the chest cavity. The surgeon was twisting a wire loop with shiny, steel, needle-nosed pliers and bending the end down into the breast bone. He realized that the whole heart bypass was completed while the studs were closing the leg incisions. How humbling that was.

"Sure, John, … and thanks."

The on-call students were encouraged to hang out in the Red ER when there were no pending admissions or surgeries. Obie was assisting Dr. Jake Dan in the ER, lancing a thrombosed hemorrhoid. His job was to hold the butt cheeks apart while Dr. Dan injected the anesthetic and did the lancing. Obie's fingers cramped as he tugged against the strong gluteal muscles of the patient, reflexively protecting his anus.

"The clots look like a cluster of grapes," noted Dr. Dan as he squeezed on the purplish bulge extruding from the anus. The blackish purple clots did look like tiny grapes to Obie. As he peeked over the field to see, a small amount of gas squeaked out of the anal sphincter. "And we're done here!" announced Dr. Dan as he quickly stepped away.

During a lull in the night, Obie looked over the newspaper article he had received from Dr. Hossaini. There was a picture of an aristocratic appearing lady and a header reading "Catherine Granger Still Sure Laetrile Was Correct Choice." She was a breast-cancer victim who had shunned conventional treatment and was doing well, supposedly due to her Laetrile therapy. When Obie called Dr. Hossaini the next morning, he told Obie he had phoned Mrs. Granger and scheduled an interview for Tuesday afternoon at four.

"Have you heard of Granger Aviation? It's an air-freight line based at Byrd Airport here in Richmond."

"Yeah, I think so."

"Well, that's her husband's company," said Dr. Hossaini.

Dr. Hossaini had Obie excused from afternoon rounds to attend the interview. Mrs. Granger was every bit as exciting as her photo. A vivacious, forty-five-year-old, classy brunette of medium build greeted them in Dr. Hossaini's office. She wore a sundress with a pastel, block-pattern print, and a plain white necklace. She recounted her story and quest for Laetrile and the metabolic-treatment regimen. This prohibited processed foods, preservatives, smoking, and alcohol. Coffee was allowed, but only as a weekly cleansing enema.

"Where did you get your Laetrile treatments?" asked Dr. Hossaini.

Obie thought to himself, *Coffee enema? How hot do you have your coffee?*

"Dr. John Donaldson is in Tennessee—one of the fourteen states where Laetrile is legal."

I wonder if she uses cream or sugar, thought Obie.

"I'll give you his address if you'd like to talk with him and review his results. After six weeks of treatment, my breast pain resolved. My breasts are full and firm, no lumps now. You're welcome to examine me if you like."

"No, that won't be helpful to us," Dr. Hossaini declined. "Our research is *in vitro*—or test tubes—and only with leukemic cells. Our results are too preliminary to make any statements. We might be interested in talking with this doctor."

"Dr. John Donaldson, Morristown, Tennessee." She handed him a business card. "Since my initial treatment, I take apricot pits twice a day for maintenance. It's legal to do that in Virginia."

This caught Obie's attention. His data was indicating positive results with the apricot-pit dialysate … but not with Laetrile itself.

In vitro cytotoxicity testing chambers for
Dialysate (DIA) and Amygdalin

Wednesday, Dr. A. B. Haynes took the M-81s through the burn ward on West 4. They were briefed on burn care, Silvadene antimicrobial dressing, the increased nutritional and fluid requirements, and the debridement tank. The tank was a stainless-steel bathtub-type structure used to soak dressings and scrub off dead tissue and scabbing.

"We usually premedicate the patients with morphine and a sedative. The scrubbing and debridement can be quite painful," Dr. Haynes explained. Obie imagined the pain, since most burn patients there had over 30 percent of their body involved.

Wednesday night was fifty-cent beer night at Parker Field, where the Richmond Braves played the Tidewater Tides. Obie took the opportunity to premedicate and sedate himself. Priscilla, even though not particularly fond of beer, drank two beers just because it was a good deal. Obie had a bit more. The electric organ sounding the charge call and the climbing march-up-the-music scale kept the excitement high during lulls in the action.

"It's a double by Rico Rodriquez!" announced the loudspeakers. The crowd cheered in response. The Braves were triumphant—

nine runs to four. Obie and Priscilla enjoyed an evening escape from the call schedule and Obie's research paper.

The next night on call, Obie revisited the Red ER. Dr. Jake Dan was assisting orthopedics, placing a forearm cast on a lady.

"This is the new fiberglass casting material," he explained to Hardy. "It's tricky to work with. You need this fiberglass-type cast padding instead of the web-roll used with plaster. It sets really fast, so we use ice water to activate it to give us time to mold it. You have to use these blue gloves and rub a Vaseline coating over them to prevent sticking to the cast." Obie thought the gloves looked like dishwashing gloves.

"Why bother with all this?" he asked.

"Well, the fiberglass is lightweight once it dries. Regular plaster feels like cement. It's also water resistant, so, if you got caught in the rain, it won't ruin your cast."

"Can you bathe with it?" he asked.

"No. The padding would get wet and wouldn't dry beneath the cast. It would stink and rot."

The patient had sustained a head injury with a concussion. She warranted admission for neurological observation. Dr. Dan did a cursory exam, placing his stethoscope at the lower edge of her breastbone or sternum.

Walking away from the patient, he explained to Obie, "The tri-ausculatory notch. You can hear breath sounds, heart sounds, and bowel sounds at the single spot," he pointed to his solar-plexus area. This was the complete opposite of the internal medicine exam that isolated the location of each heart valve and bronchopulmonary segment of the lungs. Obie picked up this patient for admission and completed his own, more thorough, exam. Her routine labs returned, and her blood sugar was high.

"Dr. Dan, Ms. Fulkerson, the concussion admission, has a glucose of 312," Obie called down to the Red ER. "Do you want to order some insulin for her?"

"Insulin? No! We're supposed to discharge her in the morning. If we start managing her diabetes, she could be in for days. Just start an IV of saline at 180 cc per hour and we'll recheck her sugar in the morning."

Obie realized this fluid was twice the amount needed for maintenance, even if this patient didn't eat or drink anything. This would essentially dilute her blood-sugar reading, as well as flushing out some glucose from her body. He felt she should have her diabetes noted and begin treatment. He persuaded the nursing staff to place her on a diabetic diet.

In the morning, her blood-sugar level was 158—not normal, but low enough to look stable for discharge from the surgery service. Also, it was low enough not to list the diagnosis of "diabetes" in her chart. Jake Dan, the IV man, was successful. Obie, however, urged her to follow up with a medical doctor, avoid sweets, and limit carbohydrates in her diet.

Saturday morning, Dr. Jake Dan covered for Dr. Springer on rounds. There were no scheduled cases on weekends. He was more enthused about the new Schwarzenegger movie, *Conan the Barbarian*, that he had seen that week than the hospitalized patients.

"In the battlefield scene, he swings this great big sword," he gestured over his head, "and chops the man's head off in one blow!" He swings his arms down. "The special effects are great! Blood spurting out of the neck!"

Obie left about one o'clock in the afternoon, after battlefield debriefing, rounds, and ward scut chores. He checked his mail before driving home, still without his bicycle. Two colored envelopes reminded him that his birthday had been the day before. There was an official-looking letter from the Virginia Society of Hematology, postmarked May 22. He opened this while still in the post office, reading quickly.

"… the chairman of the scientific program has accepted your manuscript entitled *Cytotoxicity of Normal and Leukemic Lymphocytes in Apricot Kernel Extracts* for presentation at the June, 1980, VSH meeting."

Obie was jubilant! He nearly ran to his Chevette, which

was parked on the street nearby. Street parking was a benefit of weekend rounds, since the student parking lot was a mile from the hospital. There was, allegedly, a shuttle bus to the hospital, though no M-81 had ever actually seen it. He drove straight to Priscilla's to share the news.

Priscilla was vacuuming in T-shirt, jean shorts, and bedroom slippers.

"Guess what!" he blurted.

"What?"

"They accepted my paper! I get to do the presentation at Virginia Beach!"

"Great!" She shared his excitement, knowing the work he had done and what an accomplishment this was. "I wish I could go with you."

"Yeah, me too. But I know you gotta be with your dad for the D-day thing."

Later, they celebrated his birthday and research paper with dinner at the Bella Italia.

"I can't figure a way for us to split the weekend and still be at both events," Obie stated. "They are at least four hours apart and both on Saturday morning. I could drive down by Saturday night," he offered.

"I don't know. Then we would have two cars to drive back to Richmond."

Monday found Obie with Dr. Cohen, a plastic surgeon, in the Nelson Clinic. He scrubbed in with him on a mammoplasty, or breast augmentation.

"The implants I use are saline-filled, silicone sacks," Dr. Cohen explained as they scrubbed. "Unfortunately, this lady had a leakage on the left, and the breast shrunk."

"Can you refill the sack, or do you have to replace it?" asked Obie.

"Well, since it leaked, it has to be replaced." They approached the OR table. A Caucasian female was lying supine and unconscious, with sheets covering all but her bare breasts, which were lit brightly by the overheads. Dr. Cohen pushed up the left breast and let it fall back. "See the asymmetry?"

"Uh-huh."

"She was a B cup. I enlarged her to a C cup two years ago."

"Why are both breasts prepped?" asked Obie.

"Well, she liked her new breasts so well that, since I had to replace the left implant, she wanted both breasts increased to D cups." He began to work as he talked. "Scalpel," he said, holding out his hand.

Obie watched as he reopened the prior incision scar underneath the breast and removed what looked like a cellophane sandwich bag.

"The silicone often gets wrinkles in it, and, over time, the friction of the folds rubbing together wears a hole in the liner." Obie suspected that sexual manipulation of her new "toys" had added to the friction wear.

When Dr. Cohen finished, the breasts stood up like two torpedoes, skin taught. He felt them, simultaneously squeezing them with both hands.

"Feel that!" he offered Obie, proudly. Obie timidly reached into the surgical field, feeling like he was molesting an unconscious woman. "Go ahead. Squeeze 'em," urged Cohen. They were tight and firm, but still had a fluid feel from the implants.

As they walked back to the Nelson Clinic, Obie asked, "Why would someone want to do that to their breasts?" He held the human body in highest regard, and willfully cutting and altering it for looks seemed irrational.

"Well, they like the way women's clothes fit them better and the way people look at them. They can wear more stylish fashions. It gives them more self-confidence."

"Well, I don't see it," said Obie. It seemed so superficial. Twiggy wore stylish clothes, and she was flat as a school boy.

He called Dr. Hossaini later, but he'd already known about the acceptance of their paper.

"Do you get a break this summer, Obie?" he asked.

"Well, yeah. About two weeks."

"I wrote to Dr. Donaldson, who gave Catherine Granger her Laetrile treatment. He wants us to review his charts of Laetrile-treated patients—maybe compare his results to Dr. Newell from the *New England Journal* case studies."

"That would be neat!"

"I can fund you if you can go out there."

"All right. I probably can. I'll let you know."

"Good. And congratulations on the paper. You did a good job. Don't forget to submit the tables for making the slides."

"So, your two-week summer break you plan to spend in a doctor's office in Tennessee?" asked Priscilla, hoping she had heard this wrong.

"Yeah. It's an extension of the research project. Maybe another paper." Obie felt a cold silence on the phone. "Prissy? You there?"

"Yeah," flatly, then another pause. "I think your six weeks are up." *Click.*

Forest Hill Ten Mile Run, 1979

Chapter 12
Fourth Year

r. Ali Hossaini had gotten Obie excused from surgery rotation for the weekend and paid for his room at the Cavalier Hotel. Dr. Hossaini brought his family along to stay on the rest of the week. They stayed at the original Cavalier on the hill, reopened in 1978 after being abandoned for five years. It was a 1927 grand-resort hotel, with an indoor pool, tiled promenade breezeway and porch on three sides, and a colonial styled parlor and reading room. The windows spanned ceiling to floor to catch the cool sea breezes, and green leafy plants decorated the corners. The hotel boasted that seven presidents had stayed there. It was elegant and relaxing, allowing Obie to drift back in time.

The VSH had a continental breakfast in the meeting room on Saturday morning. Obie sat through the business meeting, and, following the morning break, he was the third presenter. There were about thirty-five attendees, even less than the student honors day presentations. Also, he knew Dr. Stith, from Nassawadox, who was present. This helped lower Obie's anxiety some. He had gone over the talk in his mind numerous times, but was still apprehensive, especially with the Laetrile association. He was glad the paper only listed "apricot kernel extracts" in the title. He reviewed the cell toxicity findings, showing 97 percent and 70 percent cell lysis to leukemic cells with the DIA solution, along with the *p* values of 0.044 and 0.134.

"This effect was not seen with Laetrile or the apricot pit produced amygdalin, only with the dialysate (DIA)," he summarized. He also had a slide he had not shown Dr. Hossaini. Obie had run a liquid chromatography to see if the substances in the three test solutions were similar. Not knowing their compositions, he chose a general solvent mixture of 40 percent propyl alcohol, 50 percent acetone, and 10 percent water.

"You can see from this slide ..." He pointed to the image of a white sheet of paper. "... the Laetrile and alcohol extraction showed identical migrations. There is, however, in the extraction, a small amount of contaminant with a slower migration pattern." He pointed to a smudge lower on the sheet. "This contaminant matches the pattern of the major component of the dialysate. Both of these solutions were made from apricot pits, and the purest solution of this 'contaminant' showed the selective lysis of acute leukemic cells. Laetrile, or amygdalin, did not show this activity."

Obie looked at Dr. Hossaini, who was usually grinning or smiling, but was now actually beaming as others asked questions about extended studies on this curious substance.

In Wilmington, North Carolina, three hundred sailors in dress uniforms stood proudly on the deck of the *USS North Carolina*. In wartime, her crew numbered two thousand more, but this was a powerful display for spectators in the parking area and on the grounds. Priscilla watched from the VIP bleachers, partially shaded by a canopy, with her mother and aunt. She saw her father, Admiral Dana Watts, standing on the deck beside the bridge in his sharp, formal uniform.

He addressed the crowd. "Thirty-six years ago, we embarked on an invasion that turned the tide against the Axis forces in the European theater. The atmosphere of this historic event can be felt in General Dwight D. Eisenhower's address to the Allied forces amassed in England. I would like to play a recording of his address to the troops on the eve of the invasion."

The recording blared, "You are about to embark upon the Great Crusade, toward which we have striven these many months." It mattered little that the *USS North Carolina* did not enter the European theater, much less the Normandy D-day invasion. "... You will bring about the destruction of the German war machine, the elimination of Nazi tyranny." The crowd responded with cheers and applause. Two pair of navy jets roared overhead, leaving four white, cloud-like, vapor trail streamers.

After the ceremony, Priscilla joined her father at the reception in the Hyatt on the riverfront. Returning from the ladies room, she was approached by a young officer in crisp dress whites.

"Excuse me, miss. Weren't you just over there with Admiral Watts?"

"Well, yes I was. Why?"

"I saw you in the VIP stands at the ceremony and now here. You look kind of classy, and I wanted to meet you. I'm Petty Officer First Class James Rolland," he said, extending his hand.

"Well, Petty Officer First Class James Rolland, I'm Admiral's Daughter Priscilla Watts." She smiled, extending her hand. He was about six feet, with short, dark blond hair, his mild tan accentuated by his white uniform. Priscilla liked his gray eyes, feeling they conveyed a trusting wisdom.

The late afternoon sun setting back behind the Rudee Inlet softened and enriched the usual harsh glare of the beach. Obie was jogging back to the Cavalier Hotel along the beach sand, since the boardwalk ended a quarter of a mile shy of Forty-second street. The five-mile run had been easy, and a cool off dip in the Atlantic had been invigorating. He sat on the steps to brush the sand off his feet and put his shoes back on. A female lifeguard was dragging the last of the lounge chairs to the stack beside the stairs. Obie watched the quadriceps muscles in her thighs flexing against the resistance of the sand. The steady ocean breeze rippled the edges of the tarp cover she was pulling over the chairs. Fickle gusts of wind repeatedly blew the tarp off. Obie jumped down from the steps and held down the tarp as she bungee-corded the corners.

"Thanks," she offered. "Joe was supposed to help pack up, but he left early to chase a bikini … again."

"His loss is my gain," responded Obie.

"I saw you running earlier. How far did you go?"

"Almost to the pier and back. About five miles." Up close, her sunglasses didn't mask her features. She was an attractive girl, with black flowing long hair and a deep tan. The navy blue swimsuit fit her well, outlining her curves. "I was about to go look for a beer."

"I could use one myself," she responded.

"Well, I guess I need to go change," said Obie, giving her the chance to bow out.

"Nope. The Tiki Lounge. On the boardwalk, a couple of hotels down. I'll need to grab a shirt first."

"I'll need to grab my wallet. Meet you there in ten minutes. Oh, I'm Obie."

"Valerie," she said. "Five to ten minutes then."

On Sunday, Priscilla met Petty Officer Rolland at his military cottage lodging in Kure Beach. They spent several hours on the beach. She lay face down on her towel, with the warm sun basting her body. Rolland slowly rubbed lotion on her shoulders, back, and legs, giving her a bit of a massage in the process. She was very relaxed.

"I'll have to shower before driving back," she said.

"No problem. Use my cottage house," he offered.

She put on her shorts and polo shirt before exiting the bathroom. Petty Officer Rolland was putting on his shorts when she stepped out, affording her a glimpse of his butt shape, outlined by his white cotton briefs. He walked with his back straight, regular even steps, hinting at his military background. Neat, prim and proper, and rigid. She recalled her father's comment on Obie's loping walk.

"It's hard to get the spring out of the walk of those country plow boys," he had said.

"I'd like to see you again," said Rolland.

"Yeah, I'd like that too. Will you be in port in Virginia anytime soon?"

"Well, Monday I'm shipping out for three to four months." Priscilla was quiet, a bit numbed. "But I hope to make ensign when I'm back." This was little consolation. The flicker of a new relationship might smother over this time. "Here's how to reach me aboard ship. We get mail at each port, about every two weeks."

"Here's my number in Richmond, but I'm on call every third night," Obie said, exchanging numbers on Tiki Lounge napkins. "Watch out for sharks, now!"

"… and med students," added Valerie, smiling.

Driving back to Richmond, Obie began planning the chart review of the Laetrile treatments. He could use a helper, and Priscilla was not an option. Another med student would be great. He would cross western North Carolina to reach Tennessee. His college roommate was at Bowman-Gray Medical School in Winston-Salem. They had taken road trips to the Florida Keys and the Smokey Mountains on summer breaks. He would call David Morris as soon as he got back to the Coop.

"Dave. You up for a road trip this summer?"

"Obie? I don't know. Maybe. What's up?"

Obie filled him in on the research project and this extension. "We might get enough data to publish a paper," he offered.

"Sounds great. I'll check out my schedule and see when I'm off. I could use a break from school."

The M-81s had a class meeting in Sanger Hall. Roger "Ramjet" Walton, the president, addressed the group.

"As you know, the senior class always presents takeoffs each spring. This will cost some money, and we need to raise some funds so we don't have to pay out of pocket. Lois has found some projects we can participate in and donate the proceeds to our class fund."

Lois Jennings listed several projects, the most lucrative being the skin testing. The three-day tests paid twenty-five dollars and the three-week tests paid one hundred dollars. She suggested each M-81 volunteer for three or four short tests or one three-week test over the next six to eight months. Obie had donated plasma about once a month, whenever he needed extra cash. He also worked one night a week at Saint Luke's Hospital doing pre-op H&Ps for the orthopedic surgeons. The dermatology-research projects seemed cumbersome, but might be worth it for the class.

Obie picked up David Morris in Winston-Salem, North Carolina, along the 480-mile trek to Morristown, Tennessee. They found a room at the Mercury Court Inn for nineteen dollars a night and checked in on Sunday evening. To stretch their legs after hundreds of miles in a Chevette, they took an evening run. Eager for an early start, they arrived at Dr. Donaldson's office the next morning at eight. Obie had shared with David the testimonial of Mrs. Granger and her metabolic therapy regimen, including the coffee enemas.

"Good morning," greeted Obie to the receptionist. "I'm Obie Hardy, and this is David Morris. We're the medical students here for the record review."

"Oh, yes. We've been expecting you. Come in. Come on in the back." As she led them to a back room, she motioned toward the coffee maker. "Can I get you boys some coffee?"

Obie and David exchanged glances, recalling coffee's role in the metabolic regimen.

"No, thanks! We're fine," they answered, almost in unison.

Dr. John Donaldson was a tall, muscular man, about six two, with medium-length brown hair. He was clean shaven and wore a dress shirt with no tie.

"Obie Hardy?" he said, reaching for Obie's hand. Then, turning to David, he added, "and ..."

"David Morris," responded David. "I'm a third-year student at Bowman Gray."

"Welcome. I've pulled the charts on this table for you. There are ninety-six. I've treated 140 to 150, but many have too little information to be useful. My staff can answer any questions you have. We are currently closed for patient care, so you won't be in the way."

They began by listing chart numbers and trying to identify cancer types. The files were stashes of notes, letters, and test results, most in no discernible order—quite different from the organized hospital charts with discharge summaries. Obie and David had made little progress by the afternoon when Dr. Donaldson returned. His two office girls left at four, and he sat down with the studs to talk.

"I guess you've seen that my office is closed now."

"Well, yes, sir. We noticed," responded Obie.

"I don't have a medical license now," he continued solemnly. "I was under a lot of pressure; and I found myself drinking too much." He didn't elaborate on being ostracized by his peers for providing Laetrile; or that these dying patients had futilely hung their last hopes on him. Alcohol had helped bear these burdens, hiding him in an intoxicated fog. "Some of these patients were walking skeletons. Some had tumors protruding from their neck or chest wall. They wanted to know that they had tried *everything*. They wanted that peace of mind ... Hope, maybe." One pitiful patient had been destitute, the office staff told them later. Dr. Donaldson had boarded him in his own home and administered the treatments for free. People gossiped that he had locked the man up in his house and killed him.

"Anyway, I felt that drinking had created a hazard to my medical practice. It wasn't fair to my patients. I voluntarily resigned my license to the Board of Medicine. After being dry for six months, I requested that my license be reviewed. They have not reinstated my license and haven't given me any time course for when this may happen."

"I'm sorry," said Obie. "What are you going to do?"

"I don't know yet. I've got enough from old accounts collections and savings to keep my office staff paid for another three to six months. I'm leaving tomorrow for New Mexico. I can work on an Indian reservation there for a few weeks. I'm sorry I won't be here when you complete your review."

Obie and David were offered coffee again the next morning, at which Dave immediately dropped his pen. Bending over to pick it up, he poked his butt up in the air. He twisted his rear end a little, side to side, pretending to fumble with the fallen pen. He peeked over to Obie and, with a twinkle in his eye, answered.

"No, thanks. We're fine."

The gleaning of data from Dr. Donaldson's records generated a jumble of notes. Of the forty-five charts with usable data, there were seventeen different cancer types. To determine response rates, one needed sample populations of the same cancers. Only breast and colon cancers had multiple patients with similar disease types.

"We don't have enough information to calculate response rates, especially since most patients had also received conventional treatment regimens," said Obie.

"What about survival rates?" offered Dave.

"I guess that's the most useful data we'll get."

Before leaving for home, the studs detoured through Knoxville, less than an hour away. They visited the Parthenon, University of Tennessee, and a burlesque show at the Glass Slipper. Obie mailed Priscilla a postcard from Knoxville.

"I thought you guys were broke up," said Dave.

"Well, I don't know. I still like her . . . and she's still got my fraternity pin."

Obie had a good mix of rotations his senior year, including forensic medicine, an acting internship, infectious disease, and more obstetrics. Only the acting internship and obstetrics involved any night-call duty. He decided to utilize the extra time by increasing his running distance and try to complete the third annual Richmond Newspapers Marathon in October.

Virginia's summer humidity was well known to Obie, having worked in the hayfields much of his teenage years. There was a difference in the smell of the thick, city air that summer—most apparent when running near the James River. The odor was musty, pond-like, and later became noticeable when the faucets were running. The city water took on a slight orange tint. Radio station Q-94 reported the fragrance was due to an algae overgrowth in the river, or the "red tide". Officials assured everyone that the water was still safe to drink and that no health hazard was imposed by the phenomenon. The large, white porcelain sinks in the Pit most clearly revealed the water's orange hue.

Priscilla held a postcard from Saudi Arabia—a picture of a foreign-shaped city skyline as a backdrop to a beautiful beach. She picked up another card in her other hand with a picture of the Parthenon in Tennessee. The first read:

A. D. Priscilla Watts

I think of you often. I'll be back in the states in two more months. Hope to see you then between assignments.

She smiled and turned over the other card.

Pris,

See, it wasn't *all* work here. We saw some sights. And the coffee's fine (not like we imagined!)

Love ya, still. OB

Her face broke into a broad grin.

Back at the COOP, Obie held a sheet of paper in each hand. The left hand held the paltry review statistics on colon cancer—a measly four cases; in the right, the data from the breast cancer group—twelve women. Eighty-seven percent of the Laetrile patients had also received conventional cancer treatments. Survival rates at five years for surgically treated colon cancers were 32 percent, with this limited sample showing a comparable 25 percent. For breast cancer, mastectomies achieved 57-percent five-year survival rates, similar to the 50-percent Laetrile outcomes. These small samples remarkably mirrored current survival statistics. Obie's cell-lysis work, limited to leukemic cells, also showed Laetrile to be useless. Three cancers, three strikes against Laetrile. Nonetheless, to compose an abstract paper reporting this data, another literature search and reference list would be needed.

The infectious disease rotation was less intense than Obie's M-3 rotations, probably because it was a specialty that had a narrowed scope. They did hospital consults, attending presentations, and occasional clinic days. Most of the work involved selecting antibiotic regimens for as yet unidentified infections, tuberculosis evaluations, and determining if syphilis-screening tests were true infections or false positives. Obie had time to complete his abstract and present it to Dr. Hossaini. They sent the revised paper to Dr. Donaldson, as well as to the *Virginia Medical Monthly* journal.

Obie's jogging had reached the highest training level of his life. The blue Nikes had gotten stiff and worn, prompting his search for new footwear. Dr. Sheehan's column and book detailed the leading performance shoes as well as the use of Shoe Goo.

The goo is applied to new soles and forms an adherent rubber coating. As the shoe is worn, the goo creates a protective barrier against abrasive wear, hardening, and loss of resilience. Obies tried on several brands, ultimately choosing the twenty-nine-dollar Brooks, in navy with silver gray trim. After an initial seven-mile break-in run, he layered the yellowish tan Shoe Goo over the soles.

As the weekend-training runs exceeded two hours, he took care to route them through Byrd Park or Forest Hill Park, where drinking fountains were accessible. September city temperatures were still hot enough that running induced a sweating catharsis. Obie once measured a four-pound fluid loss after a run. By the time he had made three runs of twenty miles or more, he had become bored with running. It had become a part-time job in time commitment, consuming five to six hours a week.

Race day was a cool October morning in Shockoe Bottom where thirty-five hundred runners were gathering. Obie had urinated before driving to the downtown area, anticipating a nervous bladder effect. He ate light that morning—juice, coffee, and a Pop Tart, trusting the macaroni carbohydrate-loading regimen from the last evening. It was difficult to do warm-up stretches amid the crowd amassing at the starting line. The starting gun was anticlimactic, as the front entrants began crossing the starting line while the other runners milled about back in the crowd until the wave of movement reached them. Obie tried to begin his jog, but found himself jogging in place. He resigned to walking, crossing the start about four minutes after the gun. The first mile was slow as people jockeyed for open road areas, looking to set their pace rhythm.

"Hardy!" called a voice, and Obie looked to his left.

"Pete!" he answered, recognizing his classmate, Pete Allen.

"I didn't know you ran marathons."

"This is my first. I did run the half-marathon last year."

"This is my third. What's your pace time?"

"I don't know. I've been running eight and a half to nine-minute miles."

"All right. Just stick with me. We'll do nine-minute miles."

Obie was glad to have a veteran running partner. His confidence was reinforced. He noticed, however, Pete didn't have a race number pinned to his shirt.

"Did you lose your number?" he queried.

"Well, you know, the registration fee was thirty dollars,… and they wouldn't let you register today before the race. I'm just kinda unofficial."

The chill of the air, the excitement of the start, and the vibration from running awakened Obie's nervous bladder. At five miles, he needed to urinate. This was a distracting nuisance that gradually increased in intensity until Obie had had enough.

"I've gotta piss," he shared with Pete as they were rounding Byrd Park.

"Well, take a tree. I'll look out for you, later."

"I'll try to catch back up," he said as he left the road for a large oak tree. Other runners were answering nature's call, standing with their bellies flat up against trees so only the wet bark showed evidence of their relief.

Obie picked up his pace, a bit lighter after the eight-mile pit stop. He crossed the Nickel Bridge and rejoined Pete just before the nine-mile point. They ran together until reaching mile seventeen at Cary Street. The long, uphill leg, called "Lee's Revenge," drained tiring runners approaching "the wall." Biophysicists calculations determined that the human body had the capacity to run a maximum of eighteen miles before depleting all energy supplies and nutrients. This correlated with what runners describe as hitting "the wall," the black hole of the body's forces.

"I'm going on ahead," announced Pete, noting Obie's slowing pace. "I'll see you at the finish."

"Okay,… and thanks," puffed Obie.

"You'll do fine!" he called back over his shoulder as he charged the hill.

Obie didn't notice the wall and had done three runs over

twenty miles long without experiencing the phenomenon. Then, at mile twenty-two, Obie felt a tremendous tightening in his calves, shortening his stride. He tried to stretch his steps out, and his calf locked in a spasm, nearly knocking him to the ground. He stopped and stretched the leg, now sore as well as tight. When he pushed off to continue the race, the other calf spasmed. He knew that if he stopped to rest, he might not be able to even walk afterwards. Gatorade was available at the mile marker, and he grabbed two cups.

Potassium. Maybe it'll help, he thought. He could only take half-sized, baby steps with his rigid calf muscles, which were primed to snap into another spasm with the smallest stretch. After a half-mile, the course took on a downhill grade past Monroe Park, down Franklin Street. He spread his stride out a little, and the squeezing grip on his calves lessened slightly. His gait was still little more than a hobble.

Obie now appeared to be gaining on some runners who had slowed down. His adopted short, spastic gait was being used by others, especially the runner to his right. He recognized that red shirt.

"Pete! Smooth stride you got there!" he called.

Pete Allen looked up at Obie and smiled. "Yeah! I'm making *some* time, now!"

Obie felt his legs improving as they continued downhill. He began creeping past Pete. "I'll see you at the finish!" he called back to Pete as he shuffled on ahead.

The final two miles were better, continuing on a decline. He turned at capital square onto Ninth Street. The downhill grade grew steeper, and his legs moved automatically, his pace quickening. The twenty-six-mile point was near the Cary Street turn, and he knew he had 285 yards remaining. He began counting his steps; figuring three feet per step—probably one hundred steps remained. The crowd was thick around the finish line in Shockhoe Slip, and the course narrowed into a chute by ropes. He was at step eighty-seven when someone appeared at his side.

"You're finished! You can walk it out, now!"

Obie was dazed. The assistant was a race official, but he should still have thirteen to fifteen paces. He decided to heed the advice and walk. His legs continued on. He couldn't stop running for another fifteen steps. He wanted then to sit down. His time was 3:49:22. Sitting on a cement parking-curb marker shaded by the deck, he felt lightheaded and devoid of energy, his leg muscles tense and swollen.

"Congratulations," a soft, familiar voice sounded.

"Priscilla?" he responded, looking up and seeing her smiling face.

"You didn't think I'd miss this, after all your training, did you? How do you feel?"

"Wasted." She handed him a bottle of Gatorade. "How do I look?" he asked.

"Like a mug whump." She sat down bedside him. "I've missed you."

"Well, I've really missed you too, Priss."

"How about me treating you to dinner, tonight? You could use some nourishment."

"Well, sure. But I'll need to wash up some."

"Come on back to my place. You can bathe there."

Obie's M-4 year moved rapidly with an acting internship in North Hospital, general medicine, followed by residency interviews. He visited seven programs east, from Roanoke to Virginia Beach, and south, from Richmond to Greenville, NC. The M-81 studs had to rank their choices, and the residencies ranked the applicants. A computer would then match the program-student pairs that were the highest ranked for both, much like computer dating. Residency directors and students would communicate among themselves, seeking clues as to how each was ranking the other. Neither wished to waste a high ranking on an uninterested partner. The process climaxed on Match Day.

Match Day was in March. That Thursday afternoon, the M-81s assembled in the third-floor lecture room of Sanger Hall. Anticipatory excitement energized the chatter among the classmates, united after being scattered about for two years of clinical rotations. Hugo Siebel addressed the group as Harry Lurie posted the match lists on each side of the blackboard up front. The alphabetized rosters were attacked by the studs, eager to learn their medical career destinies.

Obie noted John Morgan hadn't battled the crowd, instead standing calmly to the rear. He was usually the first to do everything.

"Did you get your residency site?" asked Obie.

"Well, yeah. I'm on a military scholarship, you know. We've already heard of our 'assignments'. Eglin Air Force Base in Florida. Family practice."

"Oh. I got Blackstone Family Practice."

"Me, too," added Mike Rhone, joining them. "I'll be taking a pay cut to become an intern, though." In medical school, Mike had a Public Health Corps scholarship that paid a monthly stipend, and he worked externships at the North Hospital, eighth-floor detox unit and at Henrico Doctors Hospital. The internship— first year of residency—paid a salary of fifteen thousand dollars, the lavish reward for eighty to one-hundred-hour work weeks.

Each year, the senior medical class presented a satirical variety show called "Senior Take-offs." The skits, songs, dances, and film clips took over two months to prepare. The *Saturday Night Live* TV show format largely guided the M-81 production. The Cyanotic Blues Band provided the music, and there were MCV News broadcasts. Memorable songs included "Mammas Don't Let Your Babies Grow up to Be Doctors", "Fifty Ways to Leave the OR", and "R-E-S-S-E-C-T (Me)." Film excerpts showed *Mr. Bill Goes To MCV* and *Code Brown*, a training film on stool disimpaction. The audience followed Dorothy, Toto, and her entourage through episodes of their quest to see the Wizard of MCV. The Witch of the West Hospital maliciously impeded their journey, releasing the Fleas on them, until dying in the final scene as a "No Code." The entire class poured onto the stage for the finale song, "Doc," to the music of "Fame."

Obie felt a rush, an emotional high, following the final performance Thursday night. Friday, the last school day, was a lame-duck, surrealistic haze. Nothing could prohibit the graduation ceremony Saturday. Obie's mother came and spent the night at Priscilla's. They dropped Obie off Saturday morning on Leigh Street, at the lower-level entrance of the coliseum. The marquee boasted the upcoming wrestling event. The M-81s filed alphabetically onto the coliseum floor and sat in their designated section amid a sea of dental, nursing, med-tech, pharmacy, physical therapy, and PHD students. The Virginia Commonwealth University undergraduate candidates filled the majority of the seats. Visitors and guests watched from the coliseum-tiered seats, which were about one-third filled.

As the dean of VCU announced each graduate program, that group of graduates would stand in unison for recognition. The massive ceremony was grandiose, but not what Obie had been accustomed to in high school and college graduations. Their class had arranged an afternoon processional at the Grove Avenue Baptist Church in the West End. Here, each student was called by name and received a handshake and diploma from Dean Feldstein. Families and friends applauded each student's academic accomplishment at achieving a doctorate degree in medicine. The M-81s, now MDs, stood and recited the traditional Hippocratic Oath to their profession.

Grove Avenue Baptist Church, Hippocratic Oath ceremony, 1981

At Priscilla's apartment, Obie's family gathered, along with Admiral Dana Watts. Spaghetti and potato salad accompanied the champagne and beer. Mrs. Hardy had made a cake depicting Obie's twenty-year educational history in a pyramid, stair-stepped, lettering—from "Mrs. Pace's Kindergarten," to Hampden-Sydney College— "H-SC," to "MCV" at the peak.

"Oh, Obie," stated his mother, "this counts as your birthday cake, too. Six days early."

As relatives dispersed over the next day, Obie felt a lasting warmth, a glow of pride, and a sense of fulfillment. He had earned a doctorate degree, a designation attesting his level of learning and potential. Nothing had given him more satisfaction or joy ... until now. He pulled a black square box from his pocket while Priscilla was bathing and placed it under her pillow.

As they turned down the sheets, Priscilla commented, "This has been some week!"

"Yeah. The takeoffs, graduation, all the folks in town ..."

"What?" she said, puzzled, pulling the ring box from under her pillow. She looked up. "Obie?"

"I've been through the greatest experience of my life this past week. Only one thing could make it any better. Would you marry me?"

"Let's see," she stalled, seeking composure. "Two out of every three nights I'd be a wife?" Obie held his breath while she paused. She then smiled. "Yes!"

Chapter 13
Graduates

John, Samantha, and little Derrick Morgan had a long drive facing them to reach Dr. Morgan's Florida assignment. A leisurely stop in Clarksville allowed some final bonding with Obie and Priscilla. They spent a day canoeing on the lake and enjoying being outdoors again. The rural roots that they shared had made the years in classrooms and hospitals seem like prison. As Derrick napped, they sat under the shaded carport at Obie's mother's home.

John had a small marijuana stash that he couldn't take onto the military base. Obie didn't use pot, having been unimpressed with its effects when he once sampled it in the seventies in college. This celebration of friendship and parting of paths was, however, a once-in-a-lifetime event. Obie took a social puff as they passed around a joint. He handed it over to Priscilla and gazed off across the yard, noting the police cruiser in the neighbor's driveway. His mother lived beside a state trooper; he had forgotten. He suddenly realized what a drug charge would mean to his medical licensing.

His MD was only a week old and already carrying a stifling responsibility. One brilliant M-81 classmate had been expelled second year following a drug arrest.

The following morning, they stood bedside the jam-packed red Honda, rooftop baggage carrier complete. There were no words to express the deep spiritual bond Obie and John held, the shared intense academic indulgence, the sleepless nights, and the life-and-death drama that had engulfed their last four years. They embraced in the male, shoulder-hug fashion.

"Take care, 'Dr. Hardy'," bade John.

"You, too, 'Dr. Morgan'. Or is it '*Captain* Morgan'?"

He grinned. "Both."

Back in Richmond, Obie checked five days of mail and turned in his student mailbox key. A box postmarked in Tennessee was in the postage, addressed to Priscilla as well. He had her open it at her apartment. It was a silver trivet, engraved with "Obie & Priscilla Hardy" and "1981." How did he know? Obie must have mentioned his intended engagement to Dr. Ali Hossaini.

"Wow! This is great!" exclaimed Prissy. "And here's a card. 'Congratulations! Here's a little gift for you both. Good luck!' And there's a letter for you, Obie."

Obie read that Dr. John Donaldson had his license reinstated. He had submitted Obie's paper, which had listed Dr. Donaldson as a co-researcher, to a local publication. He credited this abstract as instigation for his re-licensing. Now he was challenged with rebuilding a profitable practice from the ashes of Laetrile, alcohol, and inactivity. Obie shared this with Priscilla.

"It looks like your research project did some good after all," she noted satisfactorily. "I'm sorry I wasn't as supportive as I could've been."

"Oh, no. Don't be. Your father's ceremony was the most important thing to do. I'm sorry I couldn't have made it there too."

Another letter had MCV letterhead, from the office of Dean

Feldstein. Dr. Hardy froze briefly. Had he not completed a rotation—or failed an exam? Was his degree incomplete? He tore open the envelope. He was ordered to—his "presence is necessary" at—a meeting on Friday at nine o'clock in the basement of North Hospital. No details were exposed, other than that a copy of the letter had been sent to Dr. Hossaini. Did they need him to pay back the two-hundred-sixteen-dollar expense stipend for the Morristown project? Priscilla's assurances couldn't relieve his foreboding concern.

He was the first to arrive at eight forty-five Friday. In the conference room, he fidgeted about anxiously. After an eternal ten minutes, Dr. Harold Woodson entered the room, his heme/onc attending from his West 15 medicine rotation. Obie felt that the liver-enzyme scolding might be the issue.

"Good morning, *Doctor* Hardy," he greeted, smiling.

"Good morning, Dr. Woodson," Obie replied, a little relieved by the pleasant address.

"We're still a little early. You may know that I'm the director of the Massey Cancer Center now." Obie wasn't aware of this fact, but he had no doubt that it was so. "The Center earned a prestigious designation from the National Cancer Institute in 1974 as an NCI Cancer Center. This was of great benefit in attracting research grants and getting FDA approvals for investigational drug trials."

Obie felt that his Laetrile link to MCV must have been a black mark against the cancer programs. He had little time to assimilate the potential liabilities before the other three men entered.

Dr. Ali Hossaini wore his ubiquitous smile and accompanied Dr. Stan Feldstein, dean of the MCV School of Medicine, as well as a third man. Dr. Feldstein closed the door as Dr. Hossaini presented the third gentlemen to Obie and Dr. Woodson.

"Obie, or Dr. Hardy, this is Jerry Long. He's the head of research and development for A.H. Robins Company." They shook hands and took seats around the meeting table. Dr. Feldstein began the meeting.

"It was my pleasure to arrange this meeting today. We have a proposal to ponder that may best be presented by Jerry Long from A.H. Robins."

"Thank you, Dr. Feldstein. As all of you may know, A.H. Robins has suffered recently, both in the public's eye as well as financially, thanks to the 1975 recall of the Dalkon Shield and subsequent class-action suit. We seek quick and inexpensive ways to boost our image while still pursuing quality and safety in our health care products. Dr. Hossaini and Dr. Hardy's study of leukemic cells has captured our interest. A. H. Robins is seeking a detailed proposal for *in vivo* studies using the chemical labeled DIA."

"We didn't obtain the identity of this substance, yet," stated Dr. Hossaini, looking toward Obie.

"Ah … no," began Obie, a bit stunned. "We just showed that it *wasn't* amygdalin or Laetrile." He then continued, cautiously. "It passed through a dialysis-tubing membrane, meaning that it's a small molecule, not a complex protein."

"We would next run it through the gas chromatograph in our R&D lab after reproducing a batch," stated Jerry Long. "The Massey Cancer Center has the patient population to meet our study needs."

"Especially with our proposed outreach programs," added Dr. Woodson.

Obie was awed to be witnessing this discussion. His Wednesday afternoons in a third-floor, Dooley Hospital lab no larger than a walk-in closet had led to this! And the substance of interest was a laboratory byproduct—a contaminant, so to speak, found in the attempt to produce Laetrile.

"Well," continued Long, "we need a designation for this chemical. Since you indicate that it's a molecule, we can call it *M* something."

"We presented the paper in 1980," offered Dr. Hossaini. "M-1980?"

"How about using this year?" asked Obie, presenting the most natural label he could imagine, passing on his own label. "How about M-81?"

Jerry Long smiled. "M-81 it is."